SACRIFICIAL BITE

Deborah Carter

ISBN 978-0-473-48455-2
ISBN 978-0-473-48456-9
ISBN 978-0-473-48457-6
ISBN 978-0-473-48453-3

Cover art by Steve Carter
Proofing by Spellbound

Facebook;   @debbiecarter27
Twitter;   @CDeborah6
Instagram;   @debbiecarter27
Website;   www.deborahcarterauthor.com
Email;   authordeborahcarter@gmail.com

<u>Dedication</u>

To my wonderful husband, Steve,

for those numerous cups of coffee.

(Which I forgot to drink)

Chapter one

"What the hell were you thinking? Internet hook-ups never end well, and this place is so far from town. Are you crazy?" I asked, dumbfounded as I fought to read the map she'd printed.

"Look, Jake suggested this place, so I googled it, it's the perfect spot; far enough out of town so Dad wouldn't find out, *and* I'd be safe with all the customers crowded into the place." Her voice took on that little girly whine. "Dani, please just calm down. Enjoy the ride and don't be such a buzz kill. You're making me anxious instead of excited."

"You *should* feel anxious! Take the next left. I can't believe you're meeting him at all. I mean, what do you really know about him? His name's Jake; he's 19 years old, he lives in a nearby town. It's all hearsay; people lie on the internet all the time." My voice escalated with my growing frustration. How could she not see the danger here?

Amanda sighed dramatically. I could see she was trying not to get angry with me.

"You didn't have to come with me; I could easily have driven myself out. You could be sitting right now in the library poring over your magic encyclopaedias," she replied as we turned left down the country road, the car bucking as we hit each pot-hole. Surely there must be a better road than this?

"Hmmm, it's all so fascinating; the history behind the craft has me spellbound, ha pardon the pun, and I'm definitely getting better with some of those spells; I actually had one turn ..." I shook my head and came back to the topic at hand. "Hey! Don't try and side-track me. Did you really think I'd let my baby sister drive out to the middle of nowhere to meet a total stranger? At the very least, you'll need someone to watch your back, and as you said, you don't want Dad discovering what you've been up to, so you really had no choice but to have me along once I found out about this potentially dangerous and extremely stupid plan."

"We're here!" Amanda said as she pulled the car into an empty parking space and switched the engine off. Staring through the dusty windshield, I had to admit she was right when she'd said it would be a crowded place. The small country pub was typical of hundreds of other establishments throughout Britain, with its low thatch roofing and deep-set stone walls. Coloured solar lights illuminated the near-full carpark, showering the varied style of vehicles and grassy gardens surrounding it with hues of reds, purples and blues. Music, loud with a vibrating bass spilt from the gaping doorway, its heavy oak door pushed back and stayed with an old iron doorstop. Tiny windows thrown open showed plenty of shadowed people within, swaying to the pulsing beat.

"Come on, Dani, I can't wait to meet Jake!" Amanda climbed from behind the wheel of her revolting, lime-green Austin Allegro and, reluctantly, I followed suit, warily eyeing the doorway. It was like an open mouth awaiting its prey that once inside would chew and swallow. Yeah, I had such a bad feeling about this. Amanda locked the car doors and took a few steps towards the opening. "Who knows, maybe he'll have a mate in tow for you," she tossed casually over her shoulder as she bent to pull her mini-skirt straight and to tug the non-existent creases from the soft leather of her knee-high boots before heading for the door.

With a deep breath, I hurried along after her; there was no way I was allowing her to go in alone. She may be a pain in the butt, but I loved her to pieces. My heart pounded almost painfully in my chest as we walked through the doorway. Talk about deer in the headlight scenario, people turned and stared as we stood indecisively beneath the brightest light in the room.

God, I wish Amanda had chosen a more conservative outfit for this meeting, for more than one reason. Firstly, all the male eyes raked her from head to toe, taking in the black denim mini-skirt, which showed off her long, shapely legs. Her fuchsia coloured shirt was almost spray-painted on and was held together at the front by only a couple of tiny heart-shaped buttons. Her hair was up in a high ponytail showing off her blonde and red highlights, and her well-applied make-up, hinting at the profession she'd chosen to study, accentuated her high cheekbones, the lustre in the silver eye shadow made her eyes shimmer. I had no idea she'd gotten this skilled at adding years to her young age; it made me wonder how many other times she'd dolled herself up to enter pubs and clubs. She did look stunning; although maybe a few extra inches of material would have been a good idea. My skin crawled at the looks on the guys' faces as their eyes undressed her, even in the dimly lit room, you could see the interest; fresh meat.

Secondly, it made me feel very old—spinsterish—as I stood beside her with my low-heeled boots, blue jeans, vibrant green shirt and my old faithful denim jacket that had, in all honesty, seen me through more than a couple of seasons. Although giving the room a once over, it was obvious my dress code was more the norm in the place. Amanda just plainly stood out.

A large man rose from the table nearest the door, and I watched him closely as he bent toward the unruly looking males at the table and made some comment which had them all laughing and turning to peer at us more closely.

He shuffled the few steps towards us, boots dragging along the scarred wooden floor, almost too lazy to lift his feet. The crowd turned away and went back to gyrating on the dance floor; obviously this 'fresh meat' was spoken for. Up close, the man was huge, easily over 6ft even with his neck bent at an odd angle to avoid knocking himself unconscious on the heavy wooden beams above us. His greasy brown hair hung past his ears in dirty tangles. Squinty, dark brown eyes very close together like tiny ink blots on either side of a beaked nose that had nostril hair blending into the muddy monstrosity above the thin lips, which stretched across crooked nicotine-stained teeth to create a leering smile. He wore an old weathered flannel shirt with most of the buttons missing, oil-stained jeans with the bottom cuff ragged and worn, atop scuffed steel-cap boots. He leant towards Amanda.

"Well, fuck me, aren't you just a tasty morsel? Chicky21, I presume," he breathed. The beer and smoke on his breath almost took my breath away. I hated to think how bad it must be for Amanda being just that little bit closer.

Say 'no' I thought, just say 'no', but her brain wasn't functioning quickly enough.

"Jake? You're, Jake?" she queried, her voice coming out in a much higher pitch than normal, showing me just how frightened she really was.

"Yeah, baby, come on over and join the lads." He draped a possessive arm over her shoulders and pulled her towards the table. There was only one spare seat. Pointing at me then at the empty chair, he manoeuvred himself back behind the table and pulled Amanda across his lap. I watched as she attempted to pull her mini-skirt lower to hide her very bare thighs above her boots as the other men ogled the caramel-toned tan, straight from the salon.

"You look d-different to what I imagined, Jake," she said.

"And what did you imagine, babe? Hope you aren't disappointed, 'cos I'm certainly not, you're way fuckin' hotter than your 'Chicky' icon."

"Oh," she said, her face flushing. "That's very sweet; I guess I didn't expect you to be so, I don't know ... tall, I guess. Your height makes you look older than nineteen."

"And you definitely look older than seventeen, sugar," he said with a sneer, which I think was supposed to be a grin. "Who's ya friend?"

Sitting there watching the interaction between the creep and my sister with her growing discomfort, I was kind of hoping to be ignored so I could work on a plan to get us both out of this predicament as quickly as possible.

Amanda looked at me. "This is Dani, my sister, and I see you brought some of your friends too." She looked at the five filthy, hairy-faced individuals around the table.

"Dani, a pleasure, I'm sure," Jake responded with a slight inclination of his head. "This is Max, Joe, Fig, Daz and Jay," he said as he swung his hand around the table encompassing the group of very unkempt-looking men who sat around it. They all nodded.

Drinks appeared on the table in front of us, and I wondered who'd ordered them. I hadn't seen anyone motion to the barman. I stole a glance towards the other patrons and wondered if anyone would help if I were to make a scene.

"Drink up, ladies," Jake said. I glanced at Amanda to see what she was going to do since she was, after all, underage. I could barely believe my eyes when she up-ended the glass of beer and chugged it. Where did she learn to drink like that? She wiped the foam from her upper lip and smiled at Jake, who raised his eyebrows at her and then lifted his arm to signal the barman for a refill.

I slowly took my glass from the table and cradled it, unsure that it would be wise to take a sip. Anything with bubbles gave me the hiccups and it could be very embarrassing. And besides, it looked like I would be taking over the driving if Amanda was going to drink like that.

Taking a furtive glance around the table and seeing all eyes on Amanda, or should I say on

Amanda's scanty attire, I waved my hand over my glass and murmured a few words, too quiet to be heard above the heavy thrum of the music. The colour and bubbles disappeared from my drink, and I was left to sip at the pure cold water. I didn't have time to congratulate myself on perfecting the spell as the waitress placed another drink on the sticky table, and I watched in dismay as Amanda's second beer went as quickly as her first. What the hell was she doing? Then it dawned on me, Amanda was terrified, and she was attempting to drown her fear or find some courage in the alcohol.

"Um excuse me," I said as I stood, "Just gonna spend a penny. Amanda, do you need to go?" I glared at her to understand it was my way of getting her out of a sticky situation; I'd been watching as Jake's hand moved ever closer to her breast. I wanted her off Jake's knee before he started to openly grope her in public.

"Sure, you know the old saying, 'Beer. Ya don't own it. Ya rent it,'" She giggled to herself as she placed her hands on Jake's shoulders and pushed herself off his lap and onto her feet. She wobbled as the blood rushed from her cheeks, and I hoped I could get her to the loo before she was sick.

"Hurry back now, sugar," Jake said, "my lap's getting cold already," He ran his hand across his stained jeans, and it wasn't so much his lap that he stroked over. I shuddered and watched as he picked up his glass and took a long swig. Hooking my arm through Amanda's, I half-carried, half-dragged her to the toilets. Elbowing the door open, I helped her into the cleanest of the four stalls, quickly checking the other stalls for toilet paper so I could wipe the seat. Finally bent forward, her hands planted on the edges of the cold porcelain, she brought back the two pints she'd chugged as I stood behind and held her ponytail away from her face.

"Oh God, Dani, what have I gotten us into?" She gulped, her throat stinging from the remnants of the acidic mess she'd just heaved into the bowl. "Can we leave? Is there another way out of here or do we have to go past their table? Can they see my car from where they're sitting?"

"There has to be another way out, it's a public place so legally they have to have emergency exits, and if they can see the car then we'll just have to deal with that later," I answered.

Leaning slightly into the door, I peered out through the small gap, scanning the bar. I saw Fig leave the table and head out the door. *Probably going for a leak*, I thought. Scanning the rest of the room, I spied a back door with an exit sign above it on the far side of the bar.

"Come on," I said, grasping Amanda by the hand and pulling her towards the door. "We're going to make a run for it before your boyfriend comes looking for you." Once again, I cranked the door open a smidgeon, saw Fig come back into the pub and sit back with his mates and pick up his beer.

With heads close together, the men conversed quietly, seeming to have forgotten about us; I only hoped they weren't planning on coming to find us anytime soon. We quickly slipped from the ladies' room and mingled with the sweaty, gyrating crowd on the dance floor as we made our way towards the back door and hopefully freedom. I could hardly believe our luck when we reached the exit, and like a pair of thieves, we tiptoed carefully down the pub's back steps.

The cool night air fanned my hot face, but Amanda looked sicker than she had before. Tugging on her cold fingers and bent almost double, I hurried her between the parked vehicles and onto the grassy edge of the carpark beside our car. Sneaking a furtive glance at the pub through the window of the vehicle parked beside ours, I noted that our car was partially visible to those sitting by the door. Hopefully, nobody was taking notice. Sliding the bag from Amanda's shoulder, I dug into its depth, frantically searching for the keys while all the time fighting back the fear deep in my gut that we would be discovered missing. Damn, I should have thought this out better, should have had the keys in hand as we'd made our escape instead of being stuck here like sitting ducks grasping for straws in a bag as bottomless as Mary Poppins' carpetbag.

Finally locating them caught in the lining of one of the side pockets, I fished the keys from her purse and unlocked the doors, climbed inside and frantically locked all four doors before sliding the key into the ignition. Feeling a little safer with locked doors surrounding us, we slowly pulled out of the car park onto the dark road, and only when we turned right and lost sight of the pub, did I put the lights on, hitting the full-beam button to illuminate the empty road ahead. I hit the gas pedal, and we shot down the road, safe. I sighed with relief and glanced at Amanda; her pale face was mascara-streaked as tears rained down her face as her fear finally found its release.

"I am so sorry, Dani." She gulped. "I had no idea it could go so wrong! He really seemed nice online, and his pic must have been taken years ago; he's so old."

I stayed silent, biting my tongue on the 'I told you so' threatening to spill out. I concentrated on the road, attempting to miss the deeper potholes and keeping a close vigilance on any vehicles that may be following. Suddenly, the car began to stutter, and I pumped the accelerator pedal to see if that would help but to no avail as the car shuddered once then once again before the engine cut out and we drifted to a standstill. The lights on the dashboard glowed in the darkness of the car, and my eyes were drawn to the fuel light shining brightly.

"Amanda," I said, fear clawing at my throat as I drew a deep shuddering breath. "This *was* a full tank when we left town, wasn't it?"

My fear was reflected at me from Amanda's eyes as she nodded slowly.

"Shit, shit, shit, someone's tampered with the car; it had to have been Fig when he left the pub, which means ..." My words trailed off when I caught sight of headlights drawing closer in the rear-view mirror.

Frantically, I searched my purse for my cell phone; only to discover a 'no signal' icon on the screen. Crap, crap and more crap. How were we supposed to get out of this one?

Chapter two

Amanda froze as the lights behind lit up the interior of the car, her fear taking over completely. I wasn't far behind; my heart thumped so loudly I barely heard the car pull in behind us.

Eyes frantically searched for anything we could use as a weapon, a screwdriver, a tire-iron, anything. Nothing! Nothing that would help us. My books spread out on the backseat could have been a defence if only I knew how to use them to our advantage. These magical volumes contained some dark spells, but knowing how to cast them correctly was still beyond me. I was a novice, only recently discovering my Great Grandmother had been a practising witch.

Magic, with even with the simple spells I'd mastered, was a heady experience, whetting my appetite to further my learning. I flicked my mind back to some of the spells I'd been reading, but none would assist in this situation except the protection spell, which I'd already cast; the magically infused crystal was part of an anklet hidden beneath my boot. Would it help me now? I was about to find out. My thoughts turned to Amanda; how was I to keep my little sister safe?

I turned towards her as the passenger window was suddenly filled with the looming figure of Jake, and she jumped and screamed as the door handle rattled.

"Let me in, sugar, Jakey wants a bit of sweetener," he crooned. At the same time, his hand crept along the rear door to check the handle. I glanced nervously at the little black knob to be sure it was all the way down and then jumped violently when the door behind me was also tried. Stupid, of course, he hadn't driven out on his own; he probably had all five of his goons with him. We really were in deep trouble.

Amanda looked toward me and shrieked, instinctively hiding her face as she saw the rock thrown with force at the back window mere seconds before the resounding smash and the tinkling sound of shattered glass raining down upon us. In no time at all, the car doors were being torn open and hands reaching, bruising as we were both dragged roughly from our seats and dumped on the hard, cold ground.

"What do you want from us? There's some money in my wallet, take it! Please leave us alone," I pleaded.

"I don't think so," Jake drawled as he crouched down and ran his hand over Amanda's face and down her neck. "I've wanted a piece of this for a while now; you talked the talk, baby, now it's time you deliver the goodies." His hand moved lower, cupping her breast, and she cringed as she tried to slap him away. Fig stood silently watching, and Joe licked his lips in anticipation. I jumped up not knowing what I could have done but found myself restrained by Daz and Joe one on either side of me, and Max was suddenly holding a knife to my neck as he stood in front of me almost blocking my view of my terrified sister.

Amanda's high-pitched scream pierced the darkness as Jake pushed her miniskirt up above her hips and ripped open her shirt. The two buttons pinged free as the cotton snapped, flying and landing unseen among the stones. Her fists beat at his arms and chest in a futile attempt to keep him away, and he laughed as he caught them and crushed her fingers into one of his beefy mitts. His other hand pinched and squeezed at her breasts while his knee pushed heavy and hard on her upper thighs, bruising as he forced them apart. Kneeling between them, he left her breast just long enough to unbutton the fly of his trousers and manoeuvred his body to cover my sister. Releasing her hands, he leant his forearm hard against her throat, her hands clutching, tearing at his shirt as she struggled to breathe past the pressure on her neck. His other hand slid back down to her breasts, grasping one and bringing it up to his mouth, sucking, biting at the tiny nipple leaving globules of spit to trickle into the valley between as his hand ventured lower. There came the sound of tearing fabric, and her skimpy underwear was ripped away and thrown towards his attentive audience. Joe bent and scooped them up with his free hand, dangled them in front of me for a moment before sniffing at the crotch. Grinning at the disgusted look on my face, he thrust the torn material into his pocket. "A little memento," he whispered into my ear and then turned back to watch the show.

Amanda wasn't struggling much at all now as Fig and Jay had moved forward, one at each arm as they held her spread-eagled against the gravel.

"No, no, no," she pleaded, her voice carrying her terror to me before her begging was cut short by an agony-filled scream as Jake penetrated her body. I could hear the sobs between her screams as he continued his brutal assault on her. His hips pumped fast, thrusting his rod vigorously in and out and then, with a gruff groan, he deposited his load inside of her. He glanced back at me and gave me a wink, then pulling himself free of Amanda's body, he stood up and drew his trousers back up, his now deflated cock wet against the denim. He then nodded to Fig, who quickly dropped his jeans and took over Jake's position between my sister's knees. Jake crouched, one knee pinning Amanda's arm which Fig had just released, and bent forward, roughly squeezing her bared breasts and watched with obvious enjoyment as she was taken for the second time.

Amanda screamed loudly as Fig entered her but very quickly went quiet. I couldn't bear it; tears surged down my face, fear and anger overwhelming me. My arms were held so tightly that my fingers began to tingle with the lack of blood reaching them, and I could feel an inching trail of blood from the small nick on my neck where Max's knife had pierced my skin when I tried to fight my way to her.

I watched, helpless, as Fig finished, and Jay took his place; like a tag team, they switched places. Max went next as Jake held the knife to me, and so it went on until, finally, all six had mercilessly abused her.

Amanda lay unmoving, soundless, there was no fight left in her, and my heart ached at her motionless form so savagely used and left lying on the rough ground.

Sorrow, shock and anger surged through me as the monsters released her arms and then slowly, like watching a horror movie, they stood and turned to face me. *It was my turn.* Their faces shadowed and eyes glinted evilly in the headlamps of the cars as they moved to stand in front of me.

The two goons gripping my arms suddenly propelled me forward. With feet stumbling to find purchase on the rough stones, but to no avail, I landed heavily on my side at their feet, cutting up my hands on the sharp stones and feeling the gravel rash burning a steady line down my hip. The crystal inside my boot stabbed into tender skin across my ankle bone, the blood wetting my sock.

I was so close to Amanda I could have almost reached out and touched her except Max, who loomed above me reached down to pin my arms. I took my chance. My feet shot out hard and fast, aiming for his balls. He doubled over with a howl of pain, clutching his jewels and rolling forward to land beside me on the stones. Fig and Joe reacted quicker than I thought and snatched my arms as Daz seized my legs and held them tightly. Jake's face appeared close to mine as he knelt and slapped me, then the world slowed as he held up the knife, my eyes following it as he leant over and thrust it in and up beneath Amanda's ribcage. Her gasp of pain made her almost sit up. And then with a vicious twist, the blade shredded her heart, her shoulders slumped back to the ground, and her head rolled so her eyes faced me, and I watched her life fade and disappear as blood poured from the open wound.

I screamed and received a fist to the face to silence me. It worked as I felt my lip split, and my face began to throb. The pain was nothing compared to the ache of my heartbreaking. She was dead. Oh, dear God, he'd killed my baby sister. The men holding me looked on in disbelief; rape was one thing but murder, well that was different. They were silent, all eyes on Jake as he turned and pushed Daz off my legs. Dropping the knife, he grabbed the waistband of my jeans and underwear and tugged them down to my ankles. His pants still unfastened had dropped back over his hips, and I saw his penis was rigid, pointing toward his navel. Even in the low light, I could make out the darkened colour of dried blood along his shaft, Amanda's blood.

"No-one touches my men," he growled.

Sharp stones ripped the skin on my bare buttocks as I tried in vain to kick up at him, but with my jeans wrapped around my ankles, it was impossible. Forcing my knees apart with his, Jake lay atop me, one meaty hand on each of my arms as he motioned his men away. I could feel the hard head near my entrance, and he grinned with malice as with one vicious thrust, he entered me, his body merging with mine, combining the blood of two sisters. The pain was intense, and I screamed loudly as I writhed trying to throw him off, but he was just too big, and with my ankles bound, it was impossible to move his hulk-like body. His men stood by watching, waiting their turn, listening to the symphony of my screams as Jake pounded into me. With a final thrust, he stilled, shuddered as he climaxed, his cock buried deep as he jettisoned his evil seed. His body blanketed mine briefly as he took a deep breath then with a groan, lifted his torso off me as he ground his softening genitals painfully against my groin before slipping away. He knelt above me and grinned the grin of the devil incarnate.

The rest of the gang looked from one to another, waiting for their leader to signal who was 'up to bat'. I took that half-second to find the knife lying near my hand and thrust it as hard as I could into the closest body part. Jake howled as the knife sank deeply into his thigh, and I saw his men take a step toward us.

When Jake's hands descended to my neck and began squeezing, I knew I was going to die. With the knife's hilt still in my hand, I pulled it from his flesh with a sloppy sucking sound and shifted it up in line with my breast, and then using both hands for leverage I plunged the knife up and into his chest. His hands loosened their grip on my throat, and I quickly drew in a deep breath before he had a chance to cut off my air supply again.

He rolled away from me, swearing and clutching his chest with one hand while attempting to stop the flow of blood from the wound in his thigh with the other. The men moved, two of them assisting Jake to his feet and the rest advancing on me as I scrambled awkwardly to stand. I held the bloodied knife up for them to see. Never had I felt such hatred.

"I'll kill you, all of you!" I yelled, and they stopped in their tracks looking warily at me. "I curse you all for the vile acts of tonight. By the blood on this blade, Amanda's and Jake's this I vow; you will ALL die hunted and afraid. This, I swear by the blood of my ancestors."

I wasn't at all surprised when they began to laugh and inch closer. The curse had rolled from my tongue, and even I cringed hearing it. What now? A curse had to be sealed. I cut swiftly across my already bloodied palm; the blade glowed with a white-hot light, and the blood began to sizzle. The men stopped advancing, fear showing in their eyes, and I watched in disbelief as they slowly began to back away.

"Don't listen to her," growled Jake, still holding his bleeding chest. "Once you have all fucked her, kill her. There isn't anything she can do once she's joined her slutty sister there."

No one moved. Jake staggered forward swearing and attempted to grab the knife from my hand. I swung it at him, but with my pants still around my feet, I overbalanced and found myself lurching forward. Landing heavily on my knees; the sharp stones penetrating the skin, my upper body caught by Jake's bloody hand around my neck, his fingers digging painfully into the small incision that was still oozing blood as the knife, my only lifeline, slid from my grasp and clattered to the stones.

Chapter three

The pain was agonising as his grip tightened, fingers pushed deeper into my wound slowly crushing my airway. The way it was going, I'd be dead before the others could violate me. Small mercies. I may have laughed if I'd had enough breath to do so. With breathing ragged and knees weak, tiny fireflies of light flickered in my vision as darkness began to creep across my eyes; *so, this is what it feels like to die*, I thought. A sudden chill flashed across my body, like when the winter wind blows icy rain to freeze on your skin, and the feel of goosebumps prickled my flesh. Jake's relentlessly squeezing fingers relaxed, no longer crushing, allowing me to gasp in a painful and shaky breath. My throat burned with the frigid air. Eyes which I'd kept shut against the impending darkness snapped open.

What happened? What stopped him? Was I still to be on the menu for the others to taste after all? Jake's dark eyes so close to mine were filled with absolute terror. What could he see that I couldn't? What could make a monster like Jake shake and whimper? A growl vibrated down my back. I stiffened, and the blood froze in my veins as Jake was lifted and dragged away from me, and I knew a different horror had been unleashed.

A cold hand clasped my arm, tugging me to my feet. I would have fallen again had a leaden arm not wrapped around my shoulders, effectively locking my upper arms to my sides and pinning me to a stone-hard body, and I watched in disbelief as the five men, one screaming like a teenage girl, "His eyes, oh my god, his eyes!" turned tail and sprinted to their car. The motor roared to life, and with wheels spitting up gravel, shot away disappearing into the darkness.

My gaze was drawn back to Jake as he whimpered, his face illuminated by the sickly yellow headlights of Amanda's car. His face stark, white with terror and his hands covered in his own blood from where he'd tried to staunch the crimson flow from the stab wounds I'd inflicted, now clutched at the arm that had him dangling just above the rocky ground, as he tried and failed to remove the fingers wrapped around his throat. I watched in disbelief as the new player viciously spun Jake around, so his back was prone to the monster's chest, arm pinning him in place just as I was pinned. Jake looked at me for a moment and then glanced back, locking eyes with the monster who held us.

"Stay!" The order was growled out, the voice low and dangerous. Jake didn't move a muscle as the arm released him. He swayed slightly but never ran. A hand reached for Jake's greasy hair and pulled his head forcefully to one side, the strained tendons and muscle in his neck exposed. I wanted to scream, opened my mouth to do so, but my voice deserted me, and besides, there was only the empty road and the swaying trees that would have heard me.

I was waiting to hear the crack of bone; instead, our assailant lowered his face slightly, and I watched, with saucer-wide eyes, as his jaws opened, and razor-sharp canine-like fangs lengthened from beneath his upper lip. Jake began to gabble, begging for his life just as Amanda had begged for her release, and still, he didn't try to escape.

I couldn't look away. Like seeing a car crash; you know you should turn away, but you never can. The nightmarish villain leaned in closer and with another deep, spine-chilling growl, sank those long sharp teeth deep into the taut skin on Jake's neck. His eyes bulged, widening in shock and an agony-filled howl escaped his lips, and then silence as the demon drank down the gushing blood. He sucked on that wound, swallowing, seemingly enjoying the bounty, as a bird devours sweet nectar, and then with one vicious tug, he tore Jake's throat from his body, leaving a gaping wound in his masticated neck.

No. No. No, this wasn't happening! What had I conjured? Had this demon from hell answered my call?

With my ankles still tangled in my jeans and arms held in a vice-like grip tight to my sides, my teeth were the only weapon I had left. I couldn't just die here, not without a fight, I just couldn't.

I forced my head down, my neck at some crazed angle and, with all the strength I had left, set my blunt teeth to his arm. His skin was almost leather tough, and I wondered briefly if my teeth could penetrate it. Forcing my aching jaws together, I finally gnawed through the flesh and warm fluid pulsed into my mouth.

A wash of nausea almost overcame me as my gag reflex fired, attempting to expel the metallic flavour of the blood. But with my teeth locked on his arm, vomiting was out of the question—which left only one option—I swallowed.

A tidal wave of warmth flowed over me, through me, defrosting my fear-frozen limbs as a powerful surge of energy engulfed me, giving well-needed strength to my arms. I raised scraped and painful hands to grasp his arm as I chewed harder at the warm flesh; swallowing mouthful after mouthful of the boiling elixir, intoxicating like a fine wine on an empty stomach. Images flashed through my mind; the pictures so close, so real, and almost touchable. The strobe effect echoed my heartbeat, illuminating a different scene with each pulse.

Bodies piled high, eyes staring, throats torn and bleeding. *Flash.* War scenes, the soldiers dressed in tunics on the muddy battlefield. *Flash.* A woman, dressed in a scarlet taffeta gown in a gold-lit ballroom, her head slightly to one side as she spoke to the man within whose arms she lay. *Flash, flash, flash!* Each image gruesome with blood and worse, but nothing was quite as terrifying as the last flash, as I saw myself through his eyes and his thoughts of what he intended to do.

I was vaguely aware of Jake's body as it was dropped lifeless onto the gravel with a slight thud. Then the demon turned his attention to me; watching as my mouth worked on his flesh, a slight flicker of interest showed, but then he shook his arm like I was a mosquito he wanted rid of. I flew, landing on the cold, unyielding ground. Skin scraped from my hip and shoulder, the sensation burning, but I had no time to check the damage. I turned, facing him and surprised us both with a loud giggle as he began to move stealthily toward me.

Pushing to a sitting position as the freezing stones bruised my bare bottom, I raised my face to his, and I waited.

The frosty air quickly dried the blood on my lips and chin making the skin feel tight as I lifted my tattered shirt to my lips and spat, using the dampened material in an attempted to wipe my face clean.

His face loomed close before me. My god, he was gorgeous, terrifying, but gorgeous except for those teeth. They overlapped his bottom lip just like the fangs the kids wore when they came trick-or-treating, only these weren't plastic and were stained red from the blood he had taken from Jake's throat. His hooded eyes were like dark pools, shining as the headlamps caught them. His clothes were the latest fashion and fitted his shoulders and hips like a glove. He reached for me, and I raised my hand, palm turned out towards him. He stopped.

"Kade, no! Please, don't kill me," I whispered softly.

He froze. His eyes wary as they travelled over me, taking in the shabby, out-of-season jacket, the torn and crumpled shirt before moving up to the bruise, purpling on my cheekbone. His gaze lingered on the lipstick-red tinge of his blood that, even after my spit-bath was still evident around my lips.

"How do you know my name? We've never met," he said, I could see his confusion as his brain frantically tried to retrieve a memory of a previous encounter but coming up empty. His teeth shrank back, disappearing to a normal-sized incisor as his anger began to subside.

"Umm … no," I replied. I would have most certainly remembered seeing this beautiful man before; he was hot—pits-of-hell-fire-hot at that—a gorgeous specimen that any hot-blooded woman would be attracted to, especially now that his fangs had been retracted.

I still had the urge to giggle. I'd never been drunk before, and I contemplated if this was how it felt to be intoxicated. My head felt fuzzy and light, or maybe it was shock setting in.

Kade stared down at me for a long moment before bending lower, taking my arm and pulling me none too gently to my feet. Once I found my balance, he slowly bent down again, his nose mere inches from my lady parts as he inhaled my scent and came to his conclusions as to the abuse I'd endured tonight. His proximity to my naked bottom half had my face flaming with embarrassment and yet found I was unable to move away from this man.

Reaching down, he grasped my panties and jeans, pulling them up in one smooth motion to cover my legs and buttocks before carefully buttoning and zipping my fly. Clasping my still-bleeding hand, he led me towards Amanda's car where he gently lowered me to sit sideways in the passenger seat before crouching between my feet, his hands hovering, scarcely touching my knees.

"Tell me your name!" he demanded.

"Dani."

"Do you know what I am, Dani?" he asked as his eyes bore into mine.

I couldn't look away. I'd seen enough movies to know what to call him. "Vampire," I responded smoothly as if meeting a walking, talking dead person was a daily occurrence for me.

His eyes widened, and I could see I'd shocked him with my reply. I smiled.

"And you think this because … of what I did to him?" he asked, cocking his head towards Jake's body.

"No, I saw what you were when I swallowed your blood, which is really disgusting by the way, but then I guess you're used to that. It was like … like a slideshow, snapshots of your past, showing me some extremely graphic extracts of your life. There was a woman, looking at you as you held her, she whispered your name," I said.

"What else did you see?"

"You came to protect me," I said, my head tilting slightly to the side for a better view of his face. "But you were too late! You saw what he did to me, didn't you? When you drank his blood and decided to put me out of my misery." I stuttered, "What stopped you?"

If it was at all possible, his face showed even more surprise. He stood swiftly and took a couple of steps away from me, glancing through the smashed window of the car and catching sight of my spellbooks.

"Not sure, still working on that," he finally answered. "You're a witch?" he queried.

I let out a laugh filled with bitterness.

"If I were, I wouldn't have needed saving now, would I? I dabble a little, that's all." My head seemed to be clearing slightly, and I suddenly realised I was still in some real danger here. This was all so surreal; it couldn't be true, could it? Was I stuck in some freakish nightmare? Had I fallen and hit my head? That would mean when I woke up, Amanda would still be alive, but this handsome and a little bit frightening man wouldn't really exist, and that thought bothered me.

The sound of his voice broke the silence that had fallen between us and brought me back from my reverie.

"You fear me." It was a statement, not a question this time, but I still felt compelled to answer him.

"No," I replied honestly, looking straight at him. "I should; I just saw you kill a man. I know what you are and what you could do to me, but the answer is no, I'm not scared of you. I think if you meant me harm, I'd be dead by now. I *am* wondering, however, what you plan to do with me now? I know your secret, and I could testify that you did that." I flipped a look over my shoulder at Jake lying just feet away from Amanda.

The small movement made the knife wound on my neck begin to weep. Kade inhaled deeply but caught himself before his teeth could shift and handed me a handkerchief from his pocket. I dabbed at the cut for a couple of seconds until it stopped bleeding and handed the cloth back to him. He glanced at the blood for a long spell before putting it away in his pocket.

"I don't know," Kade said. Agitated, he lifted his hand as if to run fingers through his hair and caught sight of his bloodied hand. I watched as his tongue flicked out and licked my blood from his palm, tasting, savouring. What was he seeing? With a shuddering breath, he rubbed his hand down his jacket and into the pocket. "You have to be the most unusual woman I've ever met. You've seen what I am capable of and yet you're not frightened. What on earth made you bite me?"

I glanced at his arm where my teeth had penetrated. His pale skin unblemished by my attack. "Just figured if I were going to die, I'd die fighting; leave you with a reminder of what you'd done. I see I failed at that, there isn't even a mark, just as I failed to save Amanda."

Kade looked towards my sister lying cold on the ground; her life blood drenched the torn shirt that lay splayed out beneath her like blood-covered wings.

He tentatively took my hand, helping me to my feet. Moving reluctantly with him, we walked to where she lay. He reached towards her, and I tugged his arm viciously to keep him away. He frowned at me but instantly read the emotions that raced across my face. He gently uncurled my fingers, freeing his arm from my hands and reached down to Amanda's face, closing her glassy, staring eyes.

I was suddenly drowning in my tears, and the next thing I knew, I was on my knees with my head bowed on my sister's damp, sticky chest as the sobs exploded from my lungs. How long I stayed there, I had no way of knowing. When awareness finally returned, I was freezing cold, my chest aching from the wracking sobs that attacked my body, and my legs were numb from kneeling so long on the rocky ground.

Finally, I climbed to my feet, pins and needles in my calves, running down into my toes, making me gasp in pain as the blood resumed its normal course. I collapsed back down to a squat and leant over her face and spoke to her.

"I promise you, Amanda, I will see each one of them dead, even if I have to kill them with my bare hands."

I moved then to tug at her boots, removing any creases. I covered her bared breasts where the skin had turned blue from the cold of death and finally grabbed the hem of her mini skirt to stretch it down as far as possible. I had to be strong. Taking a deep breath, I caught the smell of something. *What was that?* Then I knew. "I can smell them!" I said, glancing at Kade who stood motionless behind me. His eyes were dark and curious as he watched my reaction to the different smells.

Then he nodded. "I can too. You shouldn't be able to do that. Concentrate and tell me, are you scenting the blood and semen mixed, or can you taste the differences of the individuals involved?"

I inhaled deeply, closed my eyes and found six distinct flavours. "Different, yes. I don't know which scent belongs to which monster, but yes, I can tell each individually."

"Hmm, that's interesting." He reached and tilted my chin as he searched my eyes as if looking for answers. "I wonder what else you've inherited from ingesting my blood."

"Maybe you need to stick around and find out. Help me. Help me find these monsters so I can take those bastards down, one by one. They violated and murdered my sister, hell, one violated me, and you killed him for it, I can't let the rest get away with murder. Help me, please," I pleaded.

He regarded me for a long moment, his face a mask as he made his decision. He held his hand toward me, and I took the proffered fingers as he helped me straighten my cramped legs and regained my balance before releasing me and bending to gather Amanda's body up in his arms.

"Come along then, Dani, we must get her home before dawn pushes away our cover of darkness. I take it your car isn't going to get us to town?"

I shook my head. "No, they emptied the tank." I reached into the car and switched the headlights off, grabbed my bag and threw it over my shoulder and slammed the door.

We walked side by side down the road; Kade was cradling Amanda easily against his chest as if she weighed nothing at all.

I was aware of him watching me as I limped down the stony road. My body ached from the attack, and I was aware of pains shooting through my lower stomach from the rape. Trying to push the discomfort away, needing a distraction from the nightmare images, I began to question my rescuer.

"So, you're really a Vampire?" I said loudly, startling both of us with the volume. He raised his eyebrows at me. "I thought vamps were fictitious characters made up for scary movies. Are you how the movies depict?"

"Depends which ones you watch, they all differ," he answered. "Some are quite amusing actually. I'd love to know where they come up with some of their ideas."

"Are you really dead?"

"Do I look dead to you?" he asked.

"No, not at all, but isn't that a ... um... prerequisite or something?"

He laughed. "I guess it is, yes. I did die, but when I came back, I was stronger, faster, my senses; sight, hearing, taste, all heightened. We take blood for sustenance, but we can eat human food too; imagine eternity without a burger or a steak or mmm my favourite, cheesecake. I have a sweet fang." He laughed.

I smiled. "What else?"

"Let's see; we don't sleep in coffins or holes in the ground. I live in a nice little house and sleep in a bed. I still attend church, eat garlic, and a walk in the sun won't turn me to ash; although I'll admit, direct sunlight isn't pleasant, the UV is extremely harsh on our eyes and skin. How's that? Enough info?"

"It'll do for now," I said, shaking my head. "This is crazy; I feel like I'm in the middle of some dream. A stranger is walking me home in the early hours of the morning carrying my murdered sister, and we are discussing vampires." I stopped abruptly. "Wait a sec; you said 'we and our', how many vampires are there?"

"Thousands! We mostly live a quiet existence; humans and vampires have cohabited since the dawn of time. You wouldn't have had any idea what I was if you hadn't tasted my blood." He shook his head. "I still can't quite believe you did that. And I'm sorry that this isn't a dream. Once you come down off the high my blood has created, you'll have to face the true pain of what you've been through and the loss of your sister". It was almost as if hearing his words made me notice how exhausted I was, and when I glanced up and saw the outskirts of the town, my legs wobbled, and I stumbled, barely catching my balance in time. Kade turned into my street, following my directions to the house, and before I knew it, he was bending to lay Amanda gently on the step before straightening and turning to me as I stood almost swaying behind him.

"Dani, listen carefully, the blood you consumed will lose its capabilities in a couple of days, and then you will become normal again, be aware of your strength, you don't want to hurt anyone by accident," he said. "As to your plea for help, the answer is yes; I'll help because I wasn't in time to save you or your sister. And because I need you to know, I'm not a monster. I killed tonight because he deserved it, and you were correct in what you saw, I would have taken you too, but not to be malicious. Once I knew I'd failed you, I thought it might be a blessing to end it for you. You may still wish I had. But when I drained him, I saw you, watched you fighting for your life. I couldn't take that from you."

I listened with half an ear, almost too tired to take it all in. Capabilities? What did he mean by that?

"Capabilities?" I asked.

He let out a gruff chuckle. "That's all you heard out of that?"

"I heard you, well, most of it, but the capabilities comment got me wondering," I said.

His one brow rose, and he sighed before answering.

"Vampire blood doesn't just sit in your stomach like alcohol, Dani. It saturates your entire body. I guess you could say it's the original nanotech;

it manipulates matter on a molecular level. You'd never have made it home in your current state without it. Your strength will be quite astounding, hearing and sight more defined, and your sense of smell will have you wishing you lived in a rose garden and not among humans and animals. Remember, I saw the look on your face when you caught the scent of those animals on your sister."

"Oh," was all I could think to say. He was right. I had smelt them, and it had revolted me. I glanced at the sky when I heard the town clock begin to strike. "It's almost dawn; I'd best be getting inside with her." I glanced at Amanda. "Thanks for ..." I stopped as I turned around only to find he'd already vanished.

Taking a deep breath, I stepped around my sister to the door, unlocked it and then wedged my arms beneath Amanda's shoulders and knees, lifting her easily. Stepping back over the threshold, I kicked the door softly closed behind us. Laying her on the soft couch cushions, I stood silently staring at her broken body as dawn lit the sky outside and cast shadows along the walls. How was I going to tell Dad? I turned and slowly climbed the staircase.

Chapter four

The following two weeks had been nightmarish; during both daytime and under cover of darkness. I'd been prone to nightmares after my mother had passed away; she'd been left, bleeding to death when a hit and run driver bowled her over while she was out jogging. She left behind a grieving husband, a new-born babe, and me. The nightmares were different now; before it was my mother, lying alone, her head spilling blood and flesh like a smashed watermelon. Now they were filled with my sister's blood, flashing knives and heart-wrenching pain, and I awoke cach dawn with a scream on my lips as Amanda stood over me with a knife in her heart, her red eyes glowed unblinkingly, and from between her lips, long pointy fangs emerged ready to pierce my neck.

I was catapulted from my night terrors straight into my daytime horror, sadly from which, there was no waking, no escape. This was my life. The day of the funerals I dressed slowly, my tunic black to match the boots and the mood. How was I ever going to get through today? The undertaker's car would be here within the hour. I sat at the packed dining table, its surface littered with delicacies, quiches, savouries, sandwiches and dainty cakes, which the church women had organised for the wake, and warmed my frozen digits by wrapping them around the large mug of steaming tea as I thought back to the morning that changed everything.

The police and ambulance, sirens ear-shattering in the early morning, arrived in quick time after I placed the 999 call. Suddenly, the house was filled to overflowing with uniformed men and women. I told and retold my story as the police photographer captured my sister's body, every angle recorded, although I didn't see the point as the attack hadn't taken place at the house. Once they had all the information, a kindly policewoman helped me to one of many police vehicles outside our home and escorted me to the nearest hospital explaining along the way about the examination I would undergo. At the hospital, I was shown into an empty room and stood in the centre of a large plastic sheet and instructed to strip down. The policewoman stood near, her gloved hands holding open the individual plastic bags in which I deposited my torn and bloodied clothing, which were then sealed shut and labelled. I donned an open-backed gown and clenched a blanket around my shaking shoulders as the nurse began lining up the test boxes which contained all the requirements for a rape examination. By the time they'd finished, the boxes were filled with genital swabs, blood files, combs which had raked through my tangled hair, nail clippings and scrapings. I felt more violated than when Jake had pinned me to the ground and defiled me. Once the doctors had finished, I was finally allowed to shower and dress in hospital scrubs and then back to the room where the police continued with their questioning.

"How did you singlehandedly manage to carry Amanda home alone?"

"Adrenaline!" What else could I say? I didn't want to be committed for telling the truth.

"Why didn't you call the police to the scene?"

"No signal."

"Why didn't you only carry her until there was a signal?"

"Didn't think of it."

"Why didn't you just leave her at the scene and run for help?"

"I was in shock, for crying out loud! Hello, raped, saw my sister slaughtered. I wasn't exactly thinking straight."

It seemed like forever before the police were finally satisfied, and when I asked where she was, I was told Amanda's body had been taken to the morgue, but I couldn't see her as the medical examiner was still collecting evidence.

I arrived home alone, pushed past the police tape and let myself in. I never expected a suspected crime scene could be so messy; nothing had been cleared, debris from the ambulance crew littered the floor. I began to slowly clean until my house shone, the smell of disinfectant harsh on my nostrils.

The phone rang, and I eyed it warily, not wanting to speak to anyone, but its bell chimed over and over. Whoever was on the other end was persistent.

"What!" I barked into the receiver.

It was the nurse from the hospital, very apologetic and requesting I come in as soon as possible for another blood test; their results from the original were somehow corrupted, and they could only assume there had been some cross-contamination with another patient. They were very,

very sorry for the inconvenience. I hung up. I wouldn't be going back.

The police came one last time to assure me that everything was being done to find the perpetrators, but nothing had come to light after checking with the local trauma places and hospitals for patients presenting knife injuries I'd described inflicting.

No surprise there. I'd not mentioned Jake was dead. Nor uttered a word about the vampire, Kade.

The crime scene had been raked over, and the only evidence other than the car with its smashed window was the dark, near-black patches of dried blood and one of the little buttons, the cotton still attached that had flown from Amanda's shirt.

Jake's body was gone, and I could only surmise that Kade had gone back and removed any evidence of his death. Amanda's car had been towed and prints taken from the doors and the rock that still lay on the backseat. The police computer yielded no matching prints on file. Many of the clientele from the pub had been tracked down and interviewed, but none could give the police much information on the six bearded men. They hadn't really stood out in the crowd; hadn't caused any scene to warrant observation, although many had mentioned Amanda and described her in minute detail.

Amanda's computer was a dead end; the emails from Jake presumably sent from a phone or laptop that had no residential address attached to it. The police hazarded a guess that he'd gained access to the internet by hijacking insecure wireless connections.

As the two police officers stood to leave, the female constable thrust a bag into my hands with a strange look on her face.

"Your books," she said with a shake of her head. "The car will be held until forensics have finished. We'll let you know when you can collect it." With a nod of her head, she turned and followed her partner.

I threw the bag on the table, and the magical volumes slid from the opening. I picked one up and began thumbing through it with 'what if?' rolling around my head. 'What if there had been a spell to help me? What if I could find a way to turn back time?' I knew it was hopeless; there was nothing to be found. Suddenly alone for the first time in over 36 hours, the devastation of what happened began to take hold finally. The outing, the rape and murder. The vampire, the walk, and the moment I told Dad that Amanda was dead and he'd rushed down the stairs to stand in shocked silence as he viewed his baby daughter's broken body; his ragged breathing and the hand that crept up to hold his heart as it broke into pieces within his chest, and he fell to the floor. I'd administered CPR and dialled the emergency number, but the police and ambulance were too late to save my dad.

I stood erect and dry-eyed as I clutched the handle of the black umbrella beside the extra-deep hole and watched as the pallbearers lowered the two coffins deep into the ground, one atop the other so they would always be together.

The flat, ribbon-like rigging holding the caskets pulled free, leaving my family at the bottom, and I leaned forward and grasped a fistful of dry soil from a basket, brought it to my lips in a brief salute of farewell before letting it trickle from my numb fingers. The sound as it landed was loud on the wooden lids, and as I watched, the rain poured down, and the soil became mud and began to slide over the edges.

I turned and walked away, the silence around me giving way only to the shushing of damp leaves beneath my feet as I left the cemetery behind me.

Mourners, my father and Amanda's friends, moved around the living room; the same room that normally felt warm and inviting now felt cold and unwelcoming. I watched as they ate and drank, paying final respects to my dead family and drowning me with words of sympathy. I listened with only half an ear; my brain turned off. I just wanted them gone.

I breathed a sigh of relief when the last of them, after failing to talk me out of staying in the empty house, finally left. In my room, I changed from my funeral attire into old comfortable jeans and a jumper and then wandered through the empty house back to the living room. I stood alone as the growing darkness and silence enveloping me. So silent, I almost heard the dam around my heart splinter and crack, and I couldn't hold on anymore. As the room began to spin around me, the tears and screams of need, loneliness and grief echoed back at me from the walls, and I crumpled to the floor.

Cool, strong arms cradled me, and I leant forward against a stone-hard chest as my body shook with the outlet of my grief and trauma. Hiccupping sobs wracked my body until exhausted; I fell asleep.

<u>**Chapter five**</u>

The discomfort beneath my cheek woke me. Why was my pillow so uncomfortably hard? I struggled to open eyes that felt sore and puffy; trying to remember if I'd fallen asleep against the arm of the old couch. Wait, a couch may have arms, but not ones that wrapped around me, and I was most certainly being held. This was no couch. My eyes sprang open to discover deep, emerald-green eyes watching me intently as I lay in the circle of his arms.

"Kade? When did you ... um how long have you been here?" I husked, my throat dry and tender from crying.

"Since you called me."

"Called you? I don't even know your number," I said, pulling back to look at him properly.

"I never said you called on the telephone; you drank my blood, Dani; I felt your need through that connection; although I'm puzzled that the effects haven't worn off by now." His eyebrows pulled in at the centre as though trying to solve the mystery.

Putting my hands to his chest, I pushed away and almost toppled over the edge of my bed. That didn't seem right. Wasn't I in the living room? How did I end up on my bed, and with Kade?

"What time is it?" I asked. Glancing around the gloomy room, it appeared to be night-time as the room was in darkness except for a small light situated by my bedroom door. The drapes had been pulled, and I couldn't see even a glimmer of light from outside.

"Nineish, it's not late," he answered.

Okay, that was good, that meant he'd been here only a few hours. "I'm really sorry to have bothered you, Kade. I guess the stress of the funerals today brought home that my family really are gone." I sighed.

"The funerals weren't today, Dani, they were yesterday."

For a moment, I couldn't grasp what he was saying, and then suddenly, I understood.

"You mean I've slept through the entire day?" I squeaked horrified. "But you stayed with me?"

He nodded towards the drapes. "Lucky for me," he said. "You have good blackout curtains, and yes, you have slept around the clock."

OMG, this was crazy. I pushed to my feet and felt the room begin to tip as the floor rushed up toward me. One second, I was falling, and the next I was caught up in his arms. I gasped in shock, and he cocked his head sideways and grinned.

"Vampire! Remember?" He studied my face for a moment and said, "You're very pale; I think you could do with a good feed." Holding me close to his side, we walked slowly down the stairs and into the kitchen, where he pulled a chair back from the table and pushed me into it. Propping my elbows on the table, I rested my chin in the palms of my hands and watched the gorgeous hunk of man navigate my kitchen. Quickly finding eggs, butter, milk and cheese in the refrigerator and a frying pan below the bench; he lit the gas burner and set the pan with a dollop of butter on medium heat. Cracking the eggs into the pan, he proceeded to push them around with a spatula, breaking the yolks and adding a handful of ready grated cheese from the bag before lowering the heat and reached across the countertop to push the knob down on the toaster. I sat, stupefied, as he scraped butter on the toast and upturned the cheesy egg on top and placed it on the table before me; turning back to spoon coffee into the machine and fidgeting impatiently whilst it did its thing; finally pouring the dark, aromatic coffee into a mug and putting it beside the still-untouched plate.

"Eat!" he said and moved away to lean against the stove like an ever-watchful parent.

A smile lit my face and then a chuckle which quickly intensified until the laughter consumed me, and I was left holding my stomach and gasping for breath as tears of mirth inched down my reddened face. He simply stood, watching, waiting until my laughter slowed to a chuckle along with some very unladylike snorts, for an explanation.

"Oh God, I'm so sorry, Kade, but...." And the giggles started again. He raised his eyebrows at me, which pulled into a frown as his patience began to wear thin.

"Scrambled eggs!" I hiccupped. "It's a little, um, tame for a vampire to cook, isn't it? Wouldn't a nice red juicy steak be more appropriate?"

He smiled at me then, and I couldn't breathe. His unruly brown hair was sitting low on his collar and his fringe partially covering the arching brows above those twinkling, deep green eyes, although, from memory, I was positive they'd been hard and black as he had looked at me by the car that dreadful night. I guessed at his height in comparison to the range-hood, slightly over six feet tall and dressed in extremely snug jeans and a short-sleeved shirt which showed his biceps to perfection. But that smile! That smile lit his face like a solar flare, dazzling and memorable, his brilliant white teeth straight and even, not a fang in sight.

"Just eat, before it gets even colder, we can talk business once you've finished," he instructed.

I picked up my utensils, and after the first bite discovered I was ravenous and shovelled the food from my plate. I leaned back a little in my seat and, grabbing the basin from the bench behind me, added sugar and absently began stirring it in as he spoke.

"I've tracked down the thugs that attacked you and your sister. They all live here, around Yeovil."

"My God!" I couldn't repress the intense shudder that ran through me. "They've been that close all this time? How did you find them? The police have no leads!" I said.

"Same way you would have tracked them if you'd had the time. By scent."

I pushed back my chair a little and stood on shaky legs. "Show me!" I demanded.

He inclined his head which I took as agreement and made to move away from the table until, "Ugh um," he sounded and pointed at my coffee cup, the spoon still stirring the brown liquid. I smiled sheepishly at him. Okay, so maybe I had mastered more than one spell. "Drink it," he said. I picked the mug up and took gulps of the rich coffee, feeling it scorch my sore throat slightly with each swallow as I tried to hurry.

We headed from the kitchen, switching the lights off as we went, grabbed my jacket from the hook by the door and my car keys from the bowl on the table and locked the door behind us. He held his hand out for my keys, and I gave him a look that quite plainly said I could drive as good as he could, but he chose to ignore it and leant in to take the keys out of my hand, his fingers closing briefly over mine as he took them.

"Are you sure you're up to this?" he asked.

"No, yes," I said, shrugging my shoulders and walking to the passenger side.

He unlocked and opened my door, holding it while I settled into my seat before closing it gently. Very chivalrous; most men didn't do that anymore. I wondered just how old he was.

Chapter six

Other than the swish of the tyres eating the miles, silence filled the car. The headlights shone along the rhododendron bushes that lined the roadside, capturing the occasional flicker of yellow as the beams reflected a fox's gleaming gaze. I felt Kade's eyes on me a few times, and I finally gave in and asked, "You're watching me, why?"

He frowned. "Just trying to work you out; I can't fathom why you chose to be alone last night after the funeral. Why would you want to be on your own after such a difficult day? Surely you should have had someone there—family, friends a partner?"

"Is that your way of asking if I have a man in my life?" I asked, glancing over with a slight grin. His face stayed serious, and I harrumphed a little before responding. "Dad and Amanda were all the family I had left, and they're both gone. I don't really have close friends, my own fault," I quickly added when he glanced my way. "I was too busy studying to make any lasting friendships or relationships for that matter. I've gone out with a few guys but never found one who could compete with my love of books."

He gave me a stunned look before turning back to the road. 'With your looks," he said, "I'm guessing you had the pick of the bunch, even if they were arseholes."

What was he talking about? From the light of the dash, I studied my reflection in the window. Long black hair, thick and shining and my skin was glowing with health. After the hell I'd been through, I hadn't taken much notice of my appearance, but now I

realised I was glowing; radiant almost. I guess I'd
always been pretty to look at, never the raving beauty
that Amanda had been, but passable. I looked back at
Kade and met his dark gaze; the anger in there didn't
make sense to me. When he spoke, his voice belied
his look, the gentleness in his tone took me as much
by surprise as the words he said. "Did he hurt you?"

"What?" I asked, shocked. "He raped me!
What the hell kind of question is that?"

Kade shook his head slowly. "No, not that
monster; the man before him?"

"I don't understand; the others never touched
me; you got there before they had a chance."

"No, Dani, I'm not talking about *that* night,
I'm referring to the man you were with *before*. Did he
hurt you? Is that why you're doing this alone?"

"What?" My frown deepened. Colour me
confused. I had no idea where he was going with this
line of questioning.

Kade sighed and tried again. "Did he make it
seem special? Got what he wanted and not called
again? Have you told him?" His questions kept
coming, and I began to feel bombarded and more than
a little uneasy.

"I don't know what you're talking about," I
said, feeling uncomfortable and more than a little
offended. Was he suggesting I slept around? I'd just
told him there was no one I was involved with. "What
are you saying? Told who, what?" He glanced at me
again as I stared at him, trying to work out what he
was getting at. Anger came to my rescue. "I'll have
you know that jerk that attacked us two weeks ago—"
Two weeks was that really all it was? It felt like a

lifetime "—was my first. Jake is the only person who has ever touched me. He stole more from me than my sister's life," I choked out.

My hands shot forward to brace myself on the dashboard as the car swerved suddenly as he wrenched the steering wheel to the side and left the road, bounced onto the grass verge and slammed it into park. With the car lazily idling, he turned, one hand reaching to unclench my fingers from the dash and the other going to my long black hair and tucking it behind my ear as he stared into my eyes.

"Dani." He spoke quietly, his mouth tight as he attempted to hide his fury. My body stiffened at the expression on his face. The look in those eyes, black again, the dashboard light glinting off them. I felt a sudden fear. "You're telling me that the monster I killed took your virginity?" He almost growled the words. The thought that this beautiful woman had only experienced pain and fear was intolerable to him, her innocence snatched away by a rough evil-minded criminal, instead of by the love of a man. God, he never would have killed him so fast had he known. He should have been made to suffer, and then suffer some more, but there was no going back. What was done was done.

"Yes," I whispered, looking away and feeling the heat of shame rise to my cheeks, the shame of a woman used and abused.

"Don't!" he said, bringing my gaze back to his with his long fingers beneath my chin. "Don't ever bow your head; you have nothing to be ashamed of."

With that said, he leaned across the centre console in the car and wrapped his arms around me, holding me safe, secure, his lips on my brow so gentle it was more of a caress. My eyes closed, unsure of what I was feeling. Could I trust him? After all, I'd seen him kill a man. *But he killed to protect me,* I argued internally, and the scrunched muscles in my neck relaxed slightly. His butterfly kisses rained down from my brow, dropping to one eyelid then the other before bending his head to plant a soft but lingering kiss upon my lips.

My heart leapt, and my eyes flew open to meet his. A dark smouldering heat misted his eyes, and I pulled back, suddenly wary. He had saved my life, and for that reason alone, I trusted Kade. But this sudden tingling in my body when he kissed me was totally new to me, and it was frightening. My head told me it was wrong. I was vulnerable after what Jake had done, after losing my family, and yet even as my head screamed, 'No' the rest of my body betrayed me and said, 'Yes, yes, yes'. I wanted to belong, to be held, to be loved. I could trust him; he'd saved me. He was gorgeous, hell he was a god, and I felt so close to him; but could I trust myself? Did I really want him, or was it those last remnants of his blood in my system governing my feelings?

"I'm sorry, Dani, I shouldn't have done that." He sighed, letting his hands fall from me only to rake his hair away from his eyes, eyes that were filled with more than one kind of hunger.

Turning back to the steering wheel, he shifted into drive and pulled back out onto the road.

Casting furtive glances his way, I tried to read his expression. I wanted him to once more turn in my direction, but never once did he look my way. We drove in silence until he flicked the indicator down and pulled into the side of the road.

He pointed across the street. "That's where one of them lives," he said.

I took a deep breath and unbuckled my seatbelt. His eyes flicked to mine in a questioning glance as I climbed from the car. "I need a closer look," I explained. Keeping to the shadows, I stole closer to the one window that had a glow of light and rose up on my tiptoes to see over the window-ledge.

My heart leapt into my throat when I caught sight of one of the bastards who'd raped Amanda; "Max," I breathed as the world turned and I rocked backwards. I would have fallen if Kade hadn't appeared behind me, capturing and lowering me down to the ground, pushing my head between my knees until I was able to breathe normally again. I waved him back as I stood again, this time watching as Max checked his appearance in a large rectangular mirror built into the back of an old, yet stylish, cabinet. He ran his fingers through his hair, teasing it to stand on end. I wondered how he could look at his reflection in the mirror and not see the face of the devil that I saw when I looked at him.

There was a sudden movement beside me, and I turned to see Kade with his hand on the sill, his eyes a deep pit of iridescent ebony and his teeth shifted so I could see the sharp points from below his lip. I heard the soft growl in his throat and knew I should be terrified, and yet I wasn't. I couldn't take my eyes from him; vamped and ready to kill, he was still breath-taking.

"Not yet, Kade," I whispered and put a restraining hand on his arm. I knew he could brush me away with no effort at all, but he didn't. The growl died away as he looked at me, and his eyes and teeth morphed back. He nodded and, with a sigh, turned away from the house and pulled me after him back to the car.

"Dani, you can't do this, you're not a killer. I can't let you go in there. What if you get hurt? And if you somehow managed to exact your revenge, could you live with the guilt of taking a life?" he asked.

"I cursed them, Kade, whether they thought it was just a ruse to scare them off or if they believed every word I said, they put my sister through hell and then they killed her. I live her hell each day, and it won't go away, not until her death is avenged."

"Fine, but what do you want me to do? What's the plan of attack?" Kade asked, knowing it was pointless attempting to change my mind. I was right after all; they needed to pay for what they'd done. He just wanted to keep me safe and do the dirty work for me.

"They all had their fun with Amanda before they killed her; I intend to do the same. They need to feel the fear she felt; alone, hunted, always wondering when a killing blow will end their sorry existence." Kade's eyebrow shot upwards and disappeared beneath his fringe.

Motioning for him to start the car, we headed back towards home, my mind busy trying to come up with some ideas. By the time Kade pulled into the carport, I had semi-formulated a plan in my head.

<u>**Chapter seven**</u>

"Okay, fill me in. What's the play?" Kade said as he once again sat me at the kitchen table. I watched as he switched the coffee pot on and located the hoard of biscuits and cakes, which I had forgotten about; containers which people had left after the wake of Dad and Amanda's passing. A plate was placed in front of me with some ginger slice and Jaffa cakes. I wasn't interested and pushed it away.

"What are you trying to do to me, Kade; I'll be rolling instead of walking if you keep trying to feed me like this," I laughingly complained.

"You need to keep your strength up, Dani. I don't see things settling down for you any time soon. You've got this vendetta to fulfil and your own personal drama to attend to," he answered, but he wouldn't meet my gaze, and I wondered if he knew something I didn't.

"My plan," I said, "is to send Max a message, to let him know I am still alive and that I haven't forgotten my promise to him and his friends. I want him paranoid, forever checking over his shoulder, always wondering, waiting to see if I'll make a move."

"Great, I'm ready when you are. I've been stalking them over the past couple of weeks, so I've pretty much got their routines up here," he said, pointing to his brow.

"As much as I would like to get back out tonight, tomorrow will have to be soon enough. For some reason, I'm still tired and lightheaded when I stand; I'm just straight up exhausted, which is surprising after sleeping the day away."

Kade's brows drew into a frown as his eyes surveyed the kitchen. Pausing at the freezer, he moved across and pulled open the lid and grabbed a large slab of steak. Allowing the lid to slam behind him, he transferred his find to the microwave and punched the defrost button. I was left to watch and wonder at his actions.

"Dani, I think the reason you're feeling lightheaded has to do with your blood," he said quietly.

I looked at him closely, but he wouldn't meet my gaze. "What makes you think that? Has my drinking your blood done something to me? I'm not turning into a vampire, am I? What aren't you telling me? Come on, Kade spill, you've been dancing around something since the car."

He put his hand up to stop my barrage of questions, and I fell silent, watching him as he deftly moved the steak to a frying pan. Lighting the burner, he lightly seared it on both sides before placing it, along with some bread and butter on the plate in front of me.

"Seriously, I'm not hungry, Kade," I whined, although the tantalising aroma of the still-bloody steak was making my mouth water. What was wrong with me? I hated rare steak. Normally I ate it charcoaled, much to the disgust of Tris, down at our local steak house.

"Eat!" he ordered.

And I did. The taste was amazing; the pink juice dripped from the meat and pooled on the plate. I finished chewing the last mouthful, picked up the bread and butter and began mopping up the pink juices. Finally, with the plate clean, I sat back and looked at Kade, feeling a little ashamed when I found him studying me. Though, not enough to stop me wondering if he would find me another pack from the freezer. My face suffused with colour and I wasn't sure if it was from embarrassment or from the bloody meal I'd just consumed, either way, I felt heat burn down to my very core.

"What's going on, Kade?" I asked. "You know something, tell me."

He cocked his head towards the living room as he pushed himself away from the bench and walked from the kitchen. I followed and dropped down into my normal corner of the couch, feet pulled up close beneath my bottom and sat studying the vampire as he paced back and forth across the carpet. Finally stopping in front of me, he crouched down and took my hand, his fingers cool on my skin and his thumb nervously sliding across my knuckles.

"Dani," he said with a sigh. "There's no easy way to tell you this, and I really don't want to add to your burden, but you have to know. The reason I questioned you in the car about the men in your life, and why I was so fucking furious when you informed me that Jake stole your virginity ..." He paused, and I frowned, wondering why he would bring this up again. He glanced down at our linked hands, took a deep breath and raised his eyes to mine and quickly said, "...The reason I asked is that I can hear two heartbeats."

I stared at him, dumbstruck, not comprehending what he was trying to tell me.

"You're pregnant, Dani," he clarified for me. "When Jake raped you, he impregnated you; it's the reason you're feeling faint and lightheaded all the time."

"I'm what?" I yelled. "No!" I shook my head; there was no way a heartbeat on a foetus only sixteen days old could be heard. Impossible. "No, there must be another explanation for what you can hear, Kade. I'm sorry, but you're wrong!"

"I'm so sorry, sweetheart. I'm not wrong, I wish I were, but there's more." Running his fingers through his hair in a nervous gesture and pushing his fringe away from his eyes, he claimed my other hand and clasped it tightly.

"The child you're carrying is, at the very least, six weeks in gestation, and when you revealed to me that you weren't sexually active before the attack; well, I can only surmise the baby is a hybrid—half-human, half-vampire—for me to be able to hear it. It's all to do with timing, from when you ingested my blood and Jake's … you know," he said, his voice beginning to race a little as if he knew he was on a time limit to give all the information, a time limit before I shut him down. "A human/vampire pregnancy is a bit of an anomaly, but it has happened before. Your baby is much further along than sixteen days and will continue to grow at an abnormal speed. This pregnancy will be short compared to the usual nine months."

This wasn't happening, couldn't be happening. I watched his mouth move; why was he still talking?

What was he even on about? He must be crazy if he thought for a moment that any of this could be true.

"I know of two other hybrid pregnancies," he continued, "and both times the child was born healthy after only six to eight weeks."

I couldn't listen to this anymore. Why was he doing this to me? I snapped. "Shut up, just shut the fuck up! You're a lying piece of shit!" I screamed into his face and, pulling my hand from his grasp, reared back to slap him.

He anticipated my move, easily capturing my wrist and pinned my outstretched hand, palm forward, against his chest. Furiously, I screamed and fought against him, knowing damn well it was a losing battle, he was so much stronger than me.

Eventually, I stilled, exhaustion taking over. "Tell me it's not true," I pleaded, looking him straight in the eye and willing him to obey.

"I'm so sorry, Dani," he said.

My head shook back and forth, refusing to believe. How could this be happening to me? What had I ever done to deserve it?

My tired body began to shake as sadness and despair replaced the anger, the rage of moments ago, and he watched as I slowly accepted his truth. Removing my hand that he still held to his chest, I clutched them tight around my knees, hugging them as I rocked back and forth, like I had when I was a child and I was hurting. Kade stood over me for the longest time, watching, waiting, but I was spent. Reaching down, he plucked me from the couch and carried me ever so gently up the stairs and laid me atop the covers.

Releasing me, he turned to go when I grabbed his hand, holding on tight. I couldn't be alone right now. "Please, don't go," I whispered and pulled him down beside me.

From the centre of my bed, my gaze wandered around the room I'd grown up in, taking in all my childhood trinkets, stuffed animals on the toy hammock in the corner, the ballerinas' pink tutus fading on the wallpaper and finally the photo on the wall of my mother and father, and the tears began to flow.

Chapter eight

My tears seemed never-ending as they scoured my cheeks unchecked, hour after hour. Kade cradled me, never letting go as my tears soaked through the thin material of his shirt as we lay together on my bed. He drew a blanket up around my shoulders to help combat the shivering cold surging through my body as shock held me within its vicious grip.

"K-Kade," I hiccupped once I finally gained control of my tear ducts, and I was left sniffling and red-eyed. "Where did you come from?"

His brows furrowed. "What, you mean originally? I'm from right around here, born and bred in the South of England."

"No, that's not what I meant. That night, when Amanda and I were attacked, where did you come from? Why were you there?" I asked.

He grimaced before answering. "Well isn't that just the £100 question. Honestly, I don't know. One moment I was enjoying a nice glass of 'red', the next, an overwhelming feeling had me on my feet. I knew something was wrong, somewhere. I was out of the house and running, didn't know where I didn't know why. I wasn't hungry, didn't need to be outside. I heard screaming, ran faster until I caught a whiff of blood, *your* blood, Dani. I saw what was happening and, well, rage, like I've never felt before, took control, and you know the rest." He stroked my hair away from my damp face and kissed my cheek. "I was somehow called upon to protect you. And I failed. So, I decided it would be better for you to follow your sister. Then you bit me, and by doing so, saved your life and created a new one."

"I'm sorry if I hurt you," I mumbled. A deep rumbling sounded beneath my ear as I lay against his chest. "Are you laughing at me or growling?" I asked, not at all sure that I wanted to look up to find out.

"You didn't hurt me, sweetheart; well, no more than a little discomfort anyway, and you saw for yourself the bite left no mark."

I waited for a beat before asking what was really on my mind. "Is my baby alright?" I whispered into his shirt.

Pulling his arms from around me, he climbed off the bed, lowering my head gently to the pillow and hunkered down on the floor. Lightly placing his head on my stomach, his fingers began to tap quickly against my ribs as he duplicated the heartbeat he heard from within. Smiling up at me, he nodded. My tensed body relaxed, and I sank into the soft folds of the duvet.

Kade straightened and looked down at me with those beautiful dark eyes as his hand slipped unconsciously to the back of his neck, rubbing nervously as he said, "Dani, I need to head out for a while. Will you be okay?" He quickly added, "Not for long," when he saw my face tense.

I jerked upright, sitting like a small child, holding my knees. "Sure?" I replied, voice shaking, making my response more a question than an answer. I was afraid to be left alone. He must have caught the quiver and question in my voice because instead of leaving the room, he firmly pushed me across the bed and sank down, sitting beside my bent knees, taking and stilling my fingers as they nervously played with the cuts in my jeans. Leaning closer, his other hand stroked the dark hair away from my face, twirling his fingers into the silken strands which cascaded down over my shoulder.

Cool digits brushed against the warm skin on my neck, making me shiver in anticipation with each twirl of my hair, and I found it more and more difficult to breathe. Watching Kade, his jaw tightening, so gorgeous, so in control, as he stroked my hair and fingertips, I was mesmerised by the heat in his ever-darkening eyes. It occurred to me that he was the only man, other than my father, to ever enter my room. Boys were not allowed.

I felt intoxicated knowing that he'd spent the entire night holding me in my bed, like our own naughty little secret. Emboldened in this knowledge, I lifted my arm, bringing our entwined fingers to my lips and placed a tender kiss on his knuckles, holding my breath as his face drew ever closer to mine until I could feel his breath on my lips. Oh my god, he was going to kiss me, and I certainly wasn't going to deny him. Not when I wanted him too. Nervously, my tongue darted out to dampen suddenly dry lips as my brain, always working, made me ask. "Why do you breathe if your heart doesn't beat?"

"It makes it easier to fit in with humans," he said against my lips and then claimed them. His mouth crushed against mine, hot and hard, evoking a low moan from deep down in my throat. I didn't hold back as his tongue danced along the seam of my lips, pressing gently until they parted for him. I took his tongue into my mouth, feeling him stroke, taste, as he gently probed my tongue; a challenge to a duel, a quick nudge then snaking back, waiting to see if mine would follow. It did, happily chasing him. It was hot, intimate. I dove deeper, the kiss intensifying as my body came alive with feelings I'd never experienced. Lips still locked, he raised and held both my hands above my head as his body moved to cover mine.

Such a simple and natural act had my brain spinning, switching my burning passion to a cold shivering fear as my memories swamped me. Visions of being held and violated ran rampant, and I fought viciously against the hands holding mine, twisting my body, attempting to get free.

His lips left mine, and he instantly backed away, his body coming to lie inches away as he murmured soothing sounds, trying to calm me as his fingers gently stroked my face. My breathing slowed. I brought my gaze up to his, and my heart wrenched. He looked so guilty.

"Dani, I'm so sorry," he said, "I shouldn't have done that. I'm such an idiot; it's way too soon for you."

"Don't, Kade, please no, don't ever apologise for the kiss, not unless you hated it. I've never been kissed like that. I want you; I want to be with you. You've not done anything wrong; I promise." I took a deep breath. "I had a flashback of that night; my arms being held."

Fearing he'd up and leave, I watched him take a deep breath that would have helped calm a mortal person, but for Kade, it was a habit, a play for time to gather his thoughts, an attempt to pull himself together, to find the control he'd held for so many years.

"Hate kissing you?" He chuckled. "Impossible. Look at you. You're so beautiful, I … I'm such a fool," he choked out. "I was so caught up with my own needs; I didn't think about the ordeal you'd been through."

Reaching out, I cupped his face in my palms, bringing him closer. He sat still as a statue, not moving a muscle until I placed my lips tenderly against his parted mouth. A groan rumbled from deep in his throat and feeling encouraged I licked along the line of his mouth before thrusting inside, nudging at his tongue with my own, goading him to come back and play. Kade's hands crept around my shoulders, taking me with him as he rolled, coming to rest beneath me, ultimately giving me control. The kiss deepened, his hands sliding decadently along my spine, melding our bodies together until I could feel the full length of him. My breasts pressed against his chest and he bought his hand up to caress one hardened nipple.

I was shocked when he tore his mouth from mine.

"Dani," he almost begged. "You're killing me here all over again. I want you. No, I *need* you, but after what happened earlier, I don't want to push you."

In answer, I sat up, straddling his hips. Hooking my fingers beneath the hem of my t-shirt, I tugged it up and over my head, throwing it to the floor. Nimble fingers unbuttoned his shirt, peeling back the material to expose his chest, pale perfection broken by a smattering of hair and the solid black lines of an intricate tribal tattoo.

Tracing the dark ink, my hands took on a life of their own as they roved, reading, documenting the feel of his skin through my fingertips, smiling to myself as I located his extra-sensitive areas, feeling him tense between my thighs as I scraped my nails lightly across his skin. He bucked, almost unseating me, but he was fast to react, catching me before I could fall and pulling me back down, so I could feel the hardness imprisoned within his jeans.

Rolling the pillows beneath him, he half sat, holding me gently as he reached around my body. His hands traversed my back, running cool fingers up and down, leaving a burning trail of desire. I wriggled, and he hissed in a breath and groaned, "God, you're killing me," as he brought those talented hands up over my hips, holding me still for a long moment. He continued climbing delicately up the ladder of my rib cage until he found and unclipped the catch of my bra nestled between my breasts. Pulling it aside, I shrugged it from my shoulders, letting it slip to join my shirt on the floor.

His skin was cool to the touch, but the fire he lit inside of me burned, the heat swimming swiftly, igniting my entire body, and when he brought his head forward to capture my nipple between his lips, I thought I would combust. His lips danced from one breast to the other, his lips quickly replaced by his hands gently caressing and rolling my engorged nipples between his fingers as his lips worked their way up, nibbling, sucking the pale, slender column of my neck. Lifting me as if I weighed no more than a feather, he sat up, feet planted on the floor as my legs snaked around his hips, interlocking my feet behind his back. Tongues stroking, fingertips caressing, his chest hair sensuously tickling the smooth, silky skin of my breasts, and I knew I wanted more. No sooner had I thought it, Kade unwound my legs and gently placed me on my feet as his fingers went to my jeans. His eyes glued to mine, reading every reaction, testing my parameters, and when I made no move to stop him, he unfastened them, gripping the waistband and pushed both my jeans and panties slowly to the floor.

Nerves increased my heart rate as Kade took my hands and placed them on his jean-clad hips. He was helping me to what I wanted, yet still leaving me in control. It was sweet, and thoughtful, and funny as hell considering, right at this moment, I wasn't sure I had any control over myself; the fire in my veins was consuming, body screaming to be one with this man. When I tugged his jeans to his knees, I was surprised and delighted as his manhood bobbed free; he'd gone commando. With a quick wiggle, his jeans were down by his ankles, and he stepped out of them and kicked them away.

Oh God, he was a god. He stepped towards me then, his hands out, offering to assist me to my feet. His hard cock waved a little with the movement, distracting me momentarily. Fear struck as I remembered the pain of Jake, forcing himself into me, but I thrust it aside. That monster would not control me, ruin me any more than he'd done already. I gave Kade my hands, and in a flash, we were beneath the covers, facing one another; lips meeting, tongues gliding, hands stroking lower and lower until his fingertips fluttered across my slightly prickly mound, reminding me that I hadn't shaved in a while, but before embarrassment could overtake, he'd eased my legs apart, and his fingers found my heat. He stilled, waiting for consent, and as I deepened our kiss, I moved my hips forward, feeling his finger glide inside.

"Oh," I breathed into his mouth. I never dreamt that something could feel so wonderful. His hand moved, slowly at first and then quickened as I moaned against his lips, my hips undulating and legs shaking as I thrust down on him, needing more.

As if reading my mind, he withdrew his probing digit and rolled with me. Fisting the sheets on either side of my shoulders his body hovered above me as his member brushed at my nether regions, pulsating with want and yet he still held back, his control seemingly limitless as he waited; waited for me to freak out and push him away. Sweeping my fingers from his chest to stomach and lower still, I enclosed him in my hand and inserted the tip of his arousal. Taking a deep breath against the expected pain, I lifted my hips and encased him.

"Oh god, Dani," he groaned beside my ear as I lowered back to the bed, only to lift my hips once more, wanting to hear my name on his lips again.

Mouths locked together, lips bruising, tongues duelling, my hands roamed his back as the pleasure intensified. Nails scored down to his buttocks as I urged him deeper and faster until, until, *oh God*, I could barely breathe as I hit the pleasure threshold and, with back arched, gave a loud scream as I exploded into pieces, fragmented, flying high with the intensity of my orgasm, and then Kade was right there, growling my name over and over as he found his release. Clinging tightly to one another, we slowly floated, exhausted, back down into the mattress.

He buried his head in the pillow beside mine, bodies touching chest to toe. I wrapped my arms around him and held him close, not ever wanting this moment to end. But it did end, as a strange vibration hummed against my throat, and I jerked away from him.

Chapter nine

"What on earth? What is that?" I cried, pointing to a small, light blue crystal fastened on a leather strap around his neck.

Moving his body slightly and extracting himself, he snuggled me into his side and pulled the covers over my chilling skin. He smiled as he held the coloured stone in his hand.

"It's just a crystal," he said happily.

"Just a crystal? My crystals vibrate with energy, but nothing like that. From the smile on your face, it obviously means something to you. And why on earth did it vibrate? Is it a vampire thing? Is it special or something?" I bombarded him with questions, suddenly feeling cold at the thought that maybe it had been from a former lover or worse.

"This crystal belonged to my mother." His face went thoughtful for a moment, and I was left to wonder if he would tell me more. I lay silent and was finally rewarded when he continued. "My parents were very much in love. My mother prayed each day for the safe return of my father as he left for work. Our safety was perilous at best when he wasn't there to protect us. We had no locks for our doors, alarms to alert us to imminent danger, none of the home security we have nowadays. Life was harsh. Highwaymen, masked bandits, they would attack anyone at any time, male, female or child.

My father was friendly with an old hermit, a mystic who lived just outside of the town. Most people were frightened of her. Lina was a strange one; she looked old enough to be a grandmother but was stronger than the oxen which pulled the wagons. She knew my father to be a good man, loyal to his wife and family, and so, when he explained about my mother's constant worry, she blessed this crystal with a protection spell for him. It had to be done in secret, of course, for if it had been discovered, the woman, and probably my father too, would have been put to death; she for witchcraft and my father for collaborating with a witch and for using a magically imbued talisman. He swore that this crystal would keep Mother safe while he was away from her. She thought the real magic was the love, pure and simple, which he poured into it, and Mother felt it would always protect her.

She told me once that it hummed, sang to her, and she never took the charm from around her neck. It was unfortunate that Father never wore one himself. One day, the crystal grew silent, no hum, no song, no vibration. She knew he was gone, and she sent a couple of my father's friends and me to find him. After hours of searching, we located his body. Beaten to death, pockets emptied. The crystal never sang again."

I didn't know what to say. I was still getting my head around how hard it was to lose one's father. Gently stroking along his chest, I attempted to soothe some of the pain of all those years ago.

"My mother never got over his death. She presented me with the crystal, made me swear that I would give it to my own special love when the time came, swore it would lead me to my true love and sing again." He shook his head and watched as my hand rotated in gentle, soothing circles and said, "The crystal, Angelite, is documented to help connect you to your Guardian Angel. It's a lovely sentiment, is it not? That my father was her very own Guardian Angel? The stone supposedly connected them on a telepathic level. This crystal hasn't left my body in over three hundred years." He looked up, capturing my eyes with his. "And it's never sung to me until today."

Not knowing how to respond, I kept my eyes averted, watching instead as my fingertips followed the lines of his tattoo. When in a blink of the eye, my hand fell, dropping to the mattress as his body vanished in little more than a whisper of cool air. When I rolled over, I discovered him standing beside the bed, his eyes blacker than black as they followed the rolling lines of my body. "You are so beautiful," he said as his black eyes traversed the plains of my form. Collecting his clothing from the pile on the floor, he thrust his feet into his jeans, knowing my eyes were glued to his delectable body. My tongue snuck between my lips, and he leaned in with a quick hard kiss before turning his back on me and bent to pull the material up over his deliciously tight arse. He grinned over his shoulder and gave me a wink.

"Such a tease," I groaned. "Where are you going?"

"I'm gonna grab you a juice, and then I really need to pop out for a couple of hours," he said, striding towards the door as he buttoned his shirt.

Sliding my legs over the edge of the bed, I snared my dressing gown, attempting to push my arms into the sleeves as I stood up. The room spun, and I felt myself falling forward. Kade was there in an instant, lifting me back to the bed.

"What the hell is happening to me?" I groaned.

"It's the baby," he said, "it's fast-growing and needs more nourishment than you can supply. It's syphoning all your energy."

"But I have eaten so much already," I complained.

"It isn't hard foods that it needs, Dani," he said quietly.

I looked at him quizzically. What was he trying to say?

"The baby needs blood," he said quickly and then waited for my reaction. I didn't disappoint.

I stared at him in horror. "There is no way I am going to hunt someone so that I can drink their blood! It may be *your* way of life, and you may see it as normal, but I'm no animal. I can't rip out someone's throat. I'm not a vampire, remember?" My voice rose higher and higher as I screamed at him. Panic and worry for my unborn child, making my words harsh and hurtful.

"Human blood wouldn't help you, Dani, because as you stated, you're not a vampire. The only blood you can consume without being sick is the blood of a vampire. Mine, unless you have some other undead friend lurking around the corner."

He was angry, upset, and rightly so. I could see on his face the hurt my outburst had caused. And still, he was *the* sexiest being I'd ever laid eyes on. I hadn't meant to call him an animal or a murderer, because just looking at him, I knew he wasn't evil. He'd saved me, he looked after me, and he'd given me immeasurable pleasure. He wasn't a monster or an animal. He didn't scare me like the bogey man under the bed or the closet monster from my childhood nightmares. He was worse. He was a real walking, talking, bloodsucking vampire, and yet I was feeling guilty for putting the look of pain in his eyes.

"I'm sorry you see me as an animal," he said through gritted teeth, "but our, um, the baby needs my blood." And with that, he raised his arm to his mouth, his fangs elongated, and they slid easily into his skin. Without making eye contact, he offered me his arm.

Resignedly, I moved towards him. If his blood was what my child needed, then so be it. Inhaling deeply, I grasped his arm in both hands and pulled the bleeding wound towards my lips. I glanced once at his face wanting to apologise, but he turned away, I put my lips to his arm and drew the crimson blood into my mouth for the second time. Last time it had been in the hopes of freeing myself, and now, now it was to nourish the child his blood had helped create.

Strangely, his blood wasn't as I recalled; then, the hot gushing liquid had almost choked me. This time, this was different; tepid and sluggish. I had to gnaw at the wound, trying to keep the flow going. Why? Why was it so different? The penny dropped. Last time he'd been full, satiated by a full-grown man. Now, he was running on empty. He needed to feed to replenish his warmth and his strength, and I was holding him back. Pushing guilt aside, I concentrated on the man feeding me. The occasional flash, memories of his life came in bursts, and in every scene, blood-red coloured the landscape.

The room began to spin, and I had trouble focusing. My body floatingly light, only the solid bed beneath my knees and the hard muscles I clutched keeping me grounded. The arm I held shook, trying to dislodge my teeth, and I responded by grounding my teeth deeper.

"Enough, Dani," he barked, placing his other hand against my head and dragging his gnawed skin from between my teeth and backed away. I was left kneeling on the bed, arms outstretched, reaching for him like an alcoholic begging a passer-by for a bottle. Kade ignored me, grabbing his shoes he strode from the room without a backward glance. Numbly, I knelt with tears on my cheeks as I heard the door slam. He was gone.

Chapter ten

I lay back against the pillows, cold and lonely. The heat and passion we'd shared was gone, just like he was gone, and I was alone.

Oh God, what if he doesn't come back?

With my heart heavy and high waning; I realised I was still naked and reached once again for the dressing gown, wrapping my chilled body into the over-long garment and fastening it around my slightly-larger-than-normal belly. I headed down the stairs. My body now strong and energised, no sign of the dizziness from earlier. A quick glance around the kitchen showed he really had gone; I was alone.

Would he come back? Had I pushed him away with my stupid, short-sighted ideals? How long would it be before my baby needed more sustenance? Could I handle this pregnancy on my own?

I couldn't answer the first three, but the last, hell I knew the answer to that last question. NO! I couldn't handle this alone.

I switched on the kettle, retrieved a cup from the draining board and loaded it with coffee, sugar, and a dash of milk. Waiting for the water to boil, I leant against the bench, ankles crossed. I pushed my hand into the deep pockets and frowned.

Something cold and hard, a small stone; I pulled it from the material and gazed at the light blue crystal resting in my palm. It was the same one I'd magically imbued with the protection spell, the one that had cut into my ankle when I'd been thrown to the ground that night. I remembered now; I'd taken it from my boot while waiting for the police to arrive, rinsed it free of blood and dropped it in the pocket of my dressing gown which had been lying over the back of the couch. That memory was so clear. I wonder if that was a side effect of ingesting his blood; clarity.

The click of the kettle brought me back, and I poured the water and swirled the brown liquid around and around, leaving the spoon spinning slowly in the cup as I made my way into the lounge, placing it on the coffee table. Retrieving the television remote from the gap in the cushions, I flopped down on the couch, pulling my feet up and squeezing them beneath the twin cushion as I clicked on the television. The silent house was too much. The infomercials played in the background as I studied the shiny stone in my hand and wondered if my Angelite crystal would ever sing for me as Kade's had. And just like that, my doubts, worries and loneliness crashed over me and, like so many times in the past weeks, the tears slipped from my eyes and drenched my cheeks.

<u>**Chapter eleven**</u>

I awoke to daylight streaming in through the window, cold and stiff from sleeping on the couch. Blinking into the bright sunlight, I slowly sat up. The television still played, although the infomercials now replaced by a children's cartoon, the screen overflowing with coloured butterflies, fluttering over fields of singing flowers. With searching fingers, I located the remote and shut the telly off, the room instantly silent. I shivered, stood, and pulled my robe tighter. Bending forward with the crystal still clutched in my hand, I fastened it back into place around my ankle. Collecting the now-cold coffee, the spoon inert, the spell broken when I'd fallen asleep, I wandered into the kitchen and tossed the contents down the drain. I needed fresh coffee and aspirin.

With drums pounding in my temples, I headed to the bathroom. The dim light was gentle on my eyes and head, unlike the lounge which had been bathed in sunlight. Opening the medicine cabinet, cleverly hidden behind the mirror, I swore softly to myself as I realised my dad had put the aspirin on the top shelf, well out of my reach even if I stood on my tiptoes.

A hand on my shoulder made me squeal, and I spun around, hands up, ready to defend myself by scratching out the eyes of the intruder. Kade took both my hands in one of his, reached above me and took down the bottle of pain killers. Filling a glass with water, he handed me two little white tablets. I swallowed the pills with a swig of water and a slight toss of my head, grimacing as the pain shot through it and then smiled my thanks. Feeling incredibly shy, I pushed past him, heading back to the kitchen. I couldn't hear whether he followed or not, and I was too scared he'd see the happiness on my face if I were to look for him.

Busy, I needed to keep my hands busy. Picking up the kettle, I refilled and turned to plug it in when I came face to chest with him. He took the appliance, placed it back on its base and turned it on before turning back to me.

"You came back," I said, stating the obvious.

He nodded.

I took a harder look at him. His eyes, black as pitch last night, were now that beautiful emerald green.

"Your eyes are green. You fed!" It was a statement, not a question. He nodded again. I felt my face blanch and my breath hitch as I pictured him out hunting, stalking, and attacking people. My overactive imagination rifled through scenes from movies; had he left them for dead, weak and hurt? Were they shivering with cold and fear while they bled out in an unused building? Or maybe he'd just torn out their throat like he had Jake?

"Stop thinking before you hyperventilate," he said as if he could read my mind. "I didn't hurt anyone. A vampire's bite doesn't have to be painful. In fact, it's quite the opposite. A bite can be addictive. Some groups know of our existence; they live for our bite. We're like a drug to them. Obviously, they're compelled not to disclose our secret. The pheromones a vampire secretes are an aphrodisiac. It creates an endorphin rush like the high you get from great sex, and once they are on that high, a bite isn't painful, it's euphoric, they get high on us feeding on them. There is no pain and certainly no death. It's a win-win all around."

I hadn't known that. I'd naively thought that to feed meant pain and certain death. The enormity of what I'd accused him of last night dawned on me; embarrassment, deep red climbed my neck and filled my cheeks. "I am so sorry, Kade. I didn't know. I don't know anything," I gushed, wringing my hands together as I looked anywhere but at him.

He held his hand up, cutting my apology short. "Dani, look at me," he ordered his finger beneath my chin, raising my burning face until I was staring into his eyes. "Your assumptions were understandable. All you know is what you've seen on the television. Normally, you'd assume the worst. Please, just try and keep an open mind; if you have doubts and questions, come to me with them. I promise you; I'll do everything I can to help you through all of this."

I nodded. "I am sorry," I whispered, suddenly shy. "I was so frightened when you left, not knowing if you'd ever come back, and after we, you know…" I was blushing again. "I, um, thank you for making me feel so special." Needing to hide my embarrassment and escape those ever-watchful eyes, I moved further into him, reaching my arms around his waist and hiding my face in his shirt. He stood, unmoving for a heartbeat, and then I felt his chest rise and fall as he took in a deep breath and folded his arms around me.

"Kade," I whispered into his chest, "I'm not under your compulsion, am I?" Listening to him talk about the groupies being compelled, had me wondering. I needed to know that what I was feeling was all mine.

"No, sweetheart," he said as he ran his hands gently across my shoulders. "You have a built-in immunity from me because you ingested my blood. And while you carry this child, no other vampire can compel you either," he assured me.

Sighing with relief, I snuggled in closer. "Do you need to sleep?"

"No, I'm all good. But coffee, now *that* I could do with." Pushing me gently into a chair, he turned away to make the drinks. "What?" he said as he placed the two steaming mugs on the table, catching my surprised look. "Yes, I drink coffee." He chuckled, liberally adding sugar and cream.

He sat in the chair next to mine, and took a mouthful of the caffeinated goodness, swallowed and sighed in contentment before pulling from his pocket a pad and pen.

"Right, after I left here last night, I headed back into town and tracked our target. He hangs out at a bar by the name of ..." he checked his pad, "Bottoms Up, in Sherborne. Max was attempting to hit on a couple of girls. Blonde, shoulder-length hair, petite build."

I gasped. "Please tell me he didn't get them."

Kade chuckled. "No, someone sent them an anonymous note, informing them to steer clear as he has a rather nasty disease." He chuckled as he described their look of disgust when Max approached them, and how they turned him down with a castrating comment voiced loud and clear, about keeping his shrivelled pox-ridden prick away from them.

"I'm guessing that notebook of yours came in handy then," I said, laughing along with him. Sobering quickly, I realised the lucky escape those girls had and wished Amanda and I could have been so lucky. Quietly, I sipped at my coffee, then turned to him as an idea formulated in my head.

"We need to fuck with his head. I want him to feel afraid, violated and unsafe. We watch for him to leave the house; I'll follow him while you create a touch of chaos in his home; that way, he'll know that we have access to his safe place. Once he arrives at the bar, I'll be sure he gets a good look at me, and …"

"And then you keep your distance till I get there to cover your back," Kade interrupted. "No heroics, Dani. Don't forget; you have two to take care of now."

I nodded in agreement and drank my coffee, enjoying the comfortable silence between us. Glancing at the clock, I was amazed to discover it was well after lunchtime, and I was still in my dressing gown.

"I need to get showered and find something to wear," I said over my shoulder as I sauntered from the room and headed up the stairs.

<u>**Chapter twelve**</u>

Turning on the tap, I went to peruse my wardrobe as I waited for the water to warm up. What the hell should I wear? My clothes hung neatly on the rail; a little dull and very conservative. I really needed something that made me stand out in the crowd. Hmm, I'd think about it in the shower.

The water soothed the rest of my headache away as I massaged the shampoo and conditioner into my hair, grabbing a razor I shaved my legs before liberally adding the scented moisturising cream to a sponge and soaping my body, rinsing the bubbles away to leave my skin feeling revitalised and smooth.

Hair towelled dry and left in a messy wave around my face. I entered Amanda's room, wearing only a towel. The sight of her possessions brought a lump to my throat, and I swallowed convulsively to get it back down. Now was not the time for tears.

Running fingers over the tubes and containers in her make-up bag, I had no idea what half of it was for, so I chose what I knew; eyeshadow, mascara, and lipstick. Clutching the little collection to my chest, I hit the wardrobe to select an outfit.

I could feel her everywhere in this room; the smiling eyes in the photographs stuck to the walls, followed me, and the smell of her favourite scent still lingered, captured in the bedspread and curtains. Closing my eyes, I inhaled deeply and allowed the memories to take over.

Amanda and I lay on the bed, her arm in the pink, sticker-covered cast from when she fell from the tree a week earlier, laughing at the clothes I'd picked out to dress her Barbie doll.

I smiled to myself. Even when we were younger, she had the knack of fashion, and I didn't.

Voices from downstairs brought me reluctantly back to the now. Kade had turned on the telly, which made me wonder how long I'd been up here. Quickly grabbing the bits and bobs I'd chosen, I headed back to my room to dress.

Fifteen minutes later, I tentatively crept down the stairs, clinging for dear life to the handrail with one hand as I desperately fought with the short skirt with the other; attempting to tug the material to knee length and not just covering my upper thigh. The borrowed outfit had me feeling vulnerable, exposed as if I wasn't properly dressed, and yet all my main bits were covered. Funny how I'd felt so brave, locked in the safety of my room, the mirror showing me a whole new side to myself. A touch of make-up, light sparkly silver shadow covering my lids and the layered mascara creating extra-long, thick lashes, a luscious peachy sheen painted my lips. Now, leaving the safety of my room, the bravado waned, and I was seriously having second thoughts, until …

A low whistle greeted me as I reached the lowest step, and I relinquished the white-knuckled grip on the bannister, giving a small curtsy to thank him for his appreciation.

"You're gonna knock him dead," he said, "no pun intended."

"What are you watching?" I asked as a growl came from the TV.

"A documentary on grizzly bears," he said. "I hope you don't mind me helping myself?"

"No, of course not. What time is it anyway?" I glanced out the window and, to my surprise, saw the deepening gloom. The last of the sun almost disappearing below the fence-line.

"It's just after six-thirty; you've been upstairs most of the afternoon. I was sure you'd come down looking like a wrinkled old prune the amount of time you were in the shower, but hey you look amazing, so the time was put to good use."

Oh my god, just how long had I been lost in Amanda's room, daydreaming? It hadn't felt that long, but then I hadn't wanted to open my eyes and have her leave me again.

"Sorry it took so long, I, um, I needed clothes from Amanda's room, and I guess the time just got away on me." Glancing down at my outfit and then back to Kade, I said, "I don't own any 'come and get me' clothes."

He grinned. "I'll come and get you, clothed or not," he growled out. "You ready for this?"

I nodded. "Let's go," I said, grabbing my jacket and purse. I was halfway down the passageway when I heard him grab the keys from the kitchen table, and he still reached the door before me. I gave him one of those looks; you know the ones, the 'omg, show-off much' kind of look. Grinning, he opened the door with a flourish and, with an exaggerated bow, allowed me to precede him as he shut and locked it behind us.

A gentlemanly hand to the centre of my back assisted me to the car. He held my door, waiting for me to be seated.

Amanda's boots felt heavy and tight on my skin, and each time I bent my knees, they slipped just a little; now I knew why she was forever pulling her boots up. I settled the skirt (if you could even call it that) over my thighs as far as it would reach and turned to Kade, who was watching, eyes twinkling and lips twitching as he tried and failed to hide his amusement over my discomfort.

"Stop laughing," I growled.

With a nod and quiet chuckle, he reached and turned the key.

We drove in silence, each deep in our own thoughts. I tried to run the upcoming plan over in my head, but try as I might, within the car's close proximity, my thoughts strayed from the topic at hand and were all about the man sitting beside me. Sneaking glances his way, I watched his strong hands holding the steering wheel, and I could feel them on my body as they had been the previous night. The muscular thighs in his oh so fitting jeans just an arm's length away. Those very same thighs that were beneath my buttocks as I moved on him. That thought set my body alight, making my skin tingle, heat all over and had me squirming in my seat; the tiny little skirt riding high. Wow, this guy had really gotten under my skin.

Chapter thirteen (Kade)

Kade couldn't get out of the car fast enough. If he didn't move now, he'd be back inside her in a flash. He could smell her arousal, felt her need, or was that *his* need? What was this woman doing to him? He hadn't had a moment's rest since he went to her assistance days ago.

She was consuming his entire existence. Who was she? What had made him run to her? And what had stopped him from draining her when he discovered he was too late to save her? Why had he agreed to help her? Questions and more questions. He needed some answers.

Deep down, he knew it had nothing to do with her poor sister being brutally murdered. It was all about Dani. He had to be with her, near her, holding her, this was the only thing he was sure of.

He was lucky his heart no longer beat, for surely it would have stopped with the intensity of his desire for her last night; he should have walked away, he tried to walk away but her body called to his in a way no other had.

As she'd touched his cool skin, those warm fingers left tingling trails, her palms burned deliciously, and those lips seared deeply, bringing his long-dead feelings back to life.

When he entered the tight, volcanic heat of her body, his questions were answered, life became clear. She was his one true mate! He'd finally found that elusive part of himself, and as he lost himself inside of her, he knew he was finally complete.

To get up and leave her after they had lain together was a torture he'd never experienced. He didn't want to leave her for even a moment but knew he had to, and quickly. He needed to feed because Dani and their baby wouldn't survive if he didn't.

She didn't understand his kind, how could she? Yet when she'd attacked him with her accusations and hurled insults, he experienced a sense of betrayal, disappointed that she could think so lowly of him after what they'd shared. Feelings long since dead and buried brought back to life by his beautiful mate; not just love and desire, but the anguish and despair of disappointing the woman he loved.

He couldn't bear to watch as she fed on him, fearing she would read the pain in his eyes and think him weak. He gave her everything he had, all he could spare without endangering himself and anyone he met, and still when it came time to tear himself away as she knelt begging him for more, leaving was damn near impossible.

Sneaking back into the house in the early morning, he'd kept his distance, watched her as she slept and slipped from the room as she stirred. Her face told the story when she looked around and found she was still alone, disappointed that he hadn't returned. Later, when she'd apologised and snuggled into his chest, arms clasped so tightly, as if she'd never let go; he stood for barely a second and then his arms wrapped around her soft, warm body and held her like he'd never let her go.

As Dani showered, he attempted to keep himself under control; pacing the kitchen back and forth, over and over, but it was no good. His mind created an image, Dani wearing nothing but bubbles; those lucky glistening drops of water beading on that alabaster white skin; it was too much to bear. Leaping the stairs in a single bound, unable to remember which steps creaked, he made his way to the bathroom and entered quietly as a mouse.

This was so wrong! Spying like a stalker outside of a window, he watched as her silhouette moved behind the curtain. The way her arms raised above her head, fingers massaging her scalp, washing that silky mane which had trailed across his chest last night. The arch of her body as she leant her head back into the torrential fall of the water, the movement accentuated her rounding stomach and her perky breasts. He recalled that movement from last night, in the throes of passion, her body arching as she came, head thrown back.

This was such a bad idea. He needed to go, now.

With one last lingering, longing look, he slipped from the room, the hardness in his pants a dead giveaway to how much he wanted her. He knew, if he didn't leave now, he would be joining her, and they would be in that shower until the water ran cold, and even then, the cold water would sizzle as it touched their joined bodies.

He'd turned on the telly, the volume up loud, hoping it would block the sounds of running water above him. It worked to a certain degree, and then all that hard-won control was lost when she came down the stairs.

The sight of her in that mini skirt had him staring, like the dirty old men who ogled the club's strippers as they danced around a pole, and he felt himself harden again. He had to get himself under control.

Luckily for him, she was in a rush to get out the door, and he was able to distance himself from his wants and concentrate on getting her into the car and on their way.

From the corner of his eye, he saw her squirm in her seat, and he wondered if it was fear or excitement which had her unable to sit still? Inhaling deeply, he tasted her scent. Shit. Bad move. The onslaught of her sex-filled pheromones sent his senses reeling.

His driving became almost as erratic as his breathing would have been if he'd continued to breathe. But it was too dangerous! At times like this, being dead came in handy.

He could only imagine what thoughts were going through her head to send out such strong scents, and the more he thought, the more uncomfortable he became sitting in his tight jeans. By the time he pulled in near Max's place, he had offered her no more than a grin that was probably more of a grimace as he leapt from the car.

Chapter fourteen

Max's house was well lit when we arrived, and we'd barely parked before Kade leapt from the car and stole silently to the window, quickly disappearing into the shrubbery. He would be breaking and entering as soon as Max left. I watched intently as the occasional shadow crossed the path of light shining from the uncovered windows. I bet after tonight; he'd be pulling those curtains across.

One by one, the lights went out, and Max appeared at the front door, locked up and headed towards his car.

Sliding across to the driver's seat, headlights off, I shifted the car into gear and slowly glided away from the curb. Glancing back, I checked for signs of Kade. Was he still hiding, or had he already gained access? I could see no movement whatsoever.

Following at a short distance, I mirrored Max as he drove with a heavy foot, taking little time to approach the smaller town and pulling to the curb. Finding a vacant space a few cars back, I observed Max as he locked his vehicle, checked his reflection in his wing mirror and touched up his hair. Cautiously exiting my car, careful to be sure the inside light had been switched off, I shadowed him up the street and into the bar. A neon sign above the door read 'Bottoms Up' flashed red, blue and purple.

Edging towards an empty spot at the counter, I gingerly perched on a stool, trying hard not to think about the hundreds of strangers who'd sat here before me in similar skimpy attire, how their bare flesh had been in contact with the same cracked vinyl. It was more than a little cringeworthy.

"What can I get ya?"

"Ginger Ale thanks." I aimed a smile in his direction without taking my eyes off the prize for even a moment. Max was seated at the bar a few places down, beer already in hand. I watched as he spun around on his stool and surveyed the scene, which consisted of a few drunken women swaying on the checker-board dance floor.

Sipping my drink, I peeked through my hair, hiding in plain sight until a cold sensation ran up my spine and goosebumps pimpled my flesh, alerting me to Kade's presence. I scanned the room quickly but couldn't locate him, but I knew he was near. A breathy voice in my ear made me jump.

"Hey, babe, what have I missed?"

"Not a thing. Stalking his prey, I think. What say we get this party started?" Gulping down the last mouthful, I seized his hand. "Shall we dance?"

With his hand in mine, we wove our way out on to the dance floor. Hips swaying in time to the beat; one hand held lightly in Kade's, we moved over the black and white checked floor, slowly moving in Max's direction.

As we closed in, the music changed, the lights dimmed. Kade swayed to the slow seductive beat tucking me against his body. I allowed my cheek to rest against his chest as we moved in unison to the music. Remembering why we were here, I pushed back slightly and repositioned myself in his arms, chin fitting snuggly into the curve of his shoulder as he lowered his head, his breath playing along my ear, causing a shiver to run through me as the tempo of my heart picked up. His response was to hold me closer, one hand trailing lazily up and down my spine.

I realised with a start that Max had disappeared and turned to survey the dance floor. There he was. His arms wrapped tightly around a bottle blonde, his hands creeping down to cup her backside. I shuddered, and Kade made to move away, but I shook my head and held him close, stepping to the side a little and leading him into a half turn so he could see what had caused my reaction. A soft growl sounded from deep in his chest.

Turning, so he was once again between me and our target, I peered over his shoulder again, watching as the blonde stumbled, obviously a little drunk. Max pulled her body closer, his hips thrusting within his jeans as his fingers found the hem of her skirt and wormed underneath it. The woman smiled seductively at him and ran her fingers through his hair, mussing his spikes as she swivelled her hips suggestively against him.

The whole scene had me grimacing in disgust. Was this really the way to act in public? I watched as Max ran an eye over the other patrons, noting that they were watching him play. His fingers inched further up her skirt, and I saw his eyes take on a whole new light. He was an exhibitionist! It was really getting him off, entertaining his audience. His eyes danced over my face as he shuffled past, and I almost laughed out loud as he did a double-take, and his eyes flew back to me, wide with shock as he registered my presence.

He pushed the blonde away; she continued to sway drunkenly to the beat, barely noticing her partner had abandoned her in the middle of the floor.

"You?" he spat. "How did you escape? Where's Jake?"

Kade stopped moving and stood like a pillar of stone, not a breath or a twitch, as I pressed into him, my body shaking, adrenaline pumping as I stared over his shoulder into Max's scowling face.

"Escape?" I hissed. "Just what did I escape, Max? I didn't escape your asshole friend as he raped me. I didn't escape the nightmares every night as I replay you all raping and murdering my sister. No, I haven't escaped anything! And neither will you."

Max took a step toward me, and I heard a chuckle right beside my ear as Kade came to life and raised my arm above his head and twirled me as he spun around. We finished the movement with my back pressed intimately to the front of his body, his arms tightly binding across my chest as we both enjoyed, with sadistic pleasure, the moment Max realised who my dance partner was. His jaw dropped, and fear crept into his eyes as the colour drained from his face.

"It was you! You dredged this d-demon from hell," he stuttered.

I grinned maliciously. Let him think that. Now it was our turn for a show. I ground my backside against Kade, observing the horror on Max's face as Kade bent his head and licked a long, wet line along my neck. Tipping my head to the side, I offered him my throat, and a shiver of anticipation ran through me as he placed his lips on my exposed skin. I felt his teeth move, and I knew his fangs were showing. Max blanched, and I noted dampness appear on the inside seam of his jeans. Raising my arm, placing my hand to the back of Kade's head, I tugged his hair, manoeuvring him until his lips ran up and locked with my own. His eyes glowed, and I could feel the tip of his fangs drawing along the tongue I'd thrust between them. Then without warning, I stepped back, his hand found mine, and he spun me away from the shivering little man standing in a puddle of his own urine. I glanced back at him as we walked away, and he stared right back as Kade guided me toward the exit, his hand drifting to the centre of my back. As we reached the door, he glanced back with those menacing glowing eyes and let his hand slide down my spine to possessively cup my bottom.

Max stood frozen to the spot as he watched us walk away.

Another shiver ran through me as we exited the bar. I wasn't sure if it was the adrenaline rush wearing off or the fact that Kade's hand was still massaging my arse, sending thrills of desire coursing through my body, making my limbs weak and shaky. Or maybe it was simply the cold wind and heavy rain which had rolled in while we'd gotten hot and heavy on the dance floor. Kade caught the shiver, lifted me easily into his arms and fair flew me down the street toward the car. The wind bit through my thin top, and my knees and naked thighs goose-fleshed instantly. The car wasn't too far away, but the rain was relentless, soaking us to the skin. I aimed and beeped the auto-unlock and passed the keys to Kade as he deposited me, dripping, into the passenger seat. I'd barely fastened my belt before he turned the key and slid the heater to high.

"That was brilliant. I didn't expect him to piss himself, that was a bonus." He chortled. "Why are we leaving him alive?"

This was just the beginning. To see the fear on his face brought me one step closer to closure. 'Fear, hunted and pain' is what I'd promised. There would be no turning back.

"Whatever we do, there can be no witnesses. I will not go to jail without finishing what I promised. Their deaths must look like accidents. Only those involved will ever know the truth."

He reached over and entwined his fingers with mine, his thumb rubbing in small circles along the back of my hand, his face thoughtful. "Dani, I understand your need to avenge your sister, but murder? Are you sure you could live with yourself for ending a life? I've killed, more times than I can count. Let me do the dirty work for you, babe."

I could see the worry on his face as the car slowly cruised down the well-lit streets, and then in a blink, it was dark as we hit the outskirts and he accelerated, leaving Sherborne behind us.

I was silent for a long time, his words playing over in my head. "I'm not the same person I was this time last month, Kade. They took so much. They murdered Amanda, but they effectively killed my Dad too, and as each of them died, they took a huge part of me with them. I'm very, very sure."

Silence, broken only by the swish-swish of the windscreen wipers, the movement mirrored by my hand as I unconsciously wiped away tears I hadn't realised were falling, as always, thinking about what I'd lost left a tightness in my chest. Pulling in a deep cleansing breath, I dropped my head against the headrest and closed my eyes as the hum of the engine and hiss of the wet tires against the road lulled me into a dream space.

<u>**Chapter fifteen**</u> (Max)

Meanwhile, back at the café, Max faced an embarrassing few minutes as he attempted to escape unnoticed. No-such-luck. The patrons pointed and laughed at the wet patch seeping across the front of his pants as he sprinted for the exit. Manically searching the darkness as he fumbled with his keys, he let himself in and slammed the locks into place.

With a shaking hand, he typed and retyped his message. Finally, the words were in place, and he clicked the send button.

Help! She's come back. My place 20 minutes.

The panicked message pinged to the recipients' phones. The reaction was one of disbelief, as one by one, they stopped what they were doing. One pried himself off his couch, leaving his favourite tv program playing; another put down the tools he was working with, the new engine would have to wait; the third withdrew his body from a woman's embrace; and the last left the pizza palace without waiting for his favourite mega meat and cheese with cheesy crust, which he'd ordered and paid for.

A car, a truck, and a motorcycle hit the back roads to Yeovil.

"I'm telling you; it was her," Max yelled for the umpteenth time. "I'm not mistaken, and she was with the demon. Not a prisoner, she was '*with*' him."

The four stared at Max's ashen face; the unmistakable stench of alcohol was heavy on his breath. Could they believe this drunken asshole? Or was it the alcohol doing the talking? If he were that drunk; hell, maybe he just saw a look-a-like. Imagined the rest. They'd all been strung out since that night. Shit, Jake had really fucked up, and the fact he hadn't been seen since was a concern. The consensus was that their friend was dead, murdered by the great hulking, glowing-eyed demon. They had witnessed his immense strength as Jake had been lifted and dragged from the girl. One hand, that's all it took, one hand and Jake was dangling, feet inches from the ground.

He had growled at them as they moved to assist their friend, stopping them dead in their tracks — five grown men controlled by fear. The final straw was the two sharp canine teeth protruding that had them scrambling over each other to get in the car, running away like frightened children on Halloween. They abandoned Jake and, although each of them had done a separate drive-by, there was no sign of what occurred that night. Jake had simply vanished.

Max's eyes were wild as they flew from one friend to another, ranting, rehashing the events of his evening. His colour scarily white, the blood draining from his face as he described how the demon danced with the girl.

"Come on, he may have looked a little demonic, but I'd wager he's as human as the rest of us," Joe piped up.

"I don't give a shit whether he's human or not, he looks like a freakin' demon," Max spat.

Joe sighed, shaking his head. "Fine, we'll call him a demon. But a dancing demon?" He chuckled. "Really can't imagine that. Besides, if it was our girl; hell, think about it, Jake fucked the shit out of her, not to mention she watched her sister die. There ain't no way any chick would be out partying after that. I guarantee she'll be holed up somewhere, hiding in a corner, curtains pulled, doors locked."

"She vowed to come after us. Don't any of you remember that?" Max yelled as they began moving toward the door.

"Then we'll be vigilant," Joe said. "But right now, I'm heading home. If I'm lucky, I may even get to see the last few minutes of my program."

Daz clapped Max on the shoulder. "Get some sleep, man, get the booze out of your system, and we'll talk later, yeah?"

He followed the others to the door, and Max watched them go with fear churning in his gut. How could they not believe him? He knew what he'd seen, and he damn well wasn't drunk.

Once he was alone, Max threw the lock on the door, added the safety chain and then proceeded to check every window in every room in his home, drawing the curtains and shutting out the night. He checked in cupboards and knelt to inspect beneath his bed before finally, exhausted, he climbed in and pulled the covers high on his face, only his crazed eyes showed, darting back and forth, surveying the room.

His heart had almost stopped when he'd returned home, running from his car to his front door, panicking as he fumbled with his keys and almost dropping them in his rush to get inside. As the door finally slammed shut behind him, he'd breathed a quick sigh of relief. That was until he looked up and perused his normally tidy room. His belongings were strewn around the room, chairs upended, and his liquor cabinet emptied of its contents. It didn't take a genius to figure who'd been in his haven, his safe place. Grabbing a poker from beside the fireplace, he'd crept like a thief, going room to room as he checked for intruders, waiting for a hand to grab him around the throat and the teeth from his nightmares to rip him apart.

His mind flew back. He'd always been a brute, a known bully throughout his school years. He had been a big lad, his face pockmarked from bad teen acne. A loner, friendships had been almost non-existent, except for a handful of other bullies. Yes! He was a bully, but until that night, he'd never done anything illegal, and now he'd not only raped a woman but was a murderer by association.

These thoughts swirled around his head. Maybe he was going mad, seeing things that weren't there. God knows he'd replayed that scene in his mind a million times. The woman cursing them, the sizzling blood on the glowing blade showing crimson and black in the headlights.

***

Outside Max's place, the four mates met to discuss their latest problem.

"He's lost it!" said Joe. "Who knows what he might say or do? If he freaks out and confesses, we're all screwed."

"Then he'll have to be dealt with!" Daz replied.

They stared silently at one another, the statement creating an unease amongst them. If one of them was capable of 'silencing' Max, what was to stop that person from silencing the remaining threats?

The question was, which 'friend' would do the deed?

Were any of them safe from one another?

Ironically, the demon who could rip out their throats with his razor-sharp fangs, or the woman who'd fought and cursed them, were no longer the major threat at hand.

The hunters had become the hunted, each one a potential target.

Chapter sixteen

As the car pulled into my parking space, my eyes fluttered open. Kade appeared, opening my door, and I accepted his proffered hand. Yawning wide and loud, I trudged up the path, my fingers encased in Kade's large hand.

A person's sudden appearance near the steps had a surprised squeal leave my lips, and I stopped, stock still, unable to move or believe my eyes. Kade grimaced as I squeezed his hand, my strength so much more than ever before, thanks to his blood.

"Kade. Please tell me you see her," I whispered.

Reaching out a shaking hand, Amanda stepped toward me and pulled me into her arms.

"Amanda," I whispered, tears streaming down my cheeks.

"Dani. You need to stop this. Don't lose who you are. You've done enough. Take good care of my niece," she said with a gentle smile. "I love you. Now, wake up." Her voice dipped in pitch.

"Wake up, Dani, we're home."

Forcing heavy lids apart and taking in my surroundings, my eyes finally drew to Kade's face.

"Dani, what's wrong? You're crying."

"Oh, it wasn't real." I sniffed, swatting at the tears on my cheeks. "It was just a dream."

"Do you want to tell me about it?" Kade queried.

I nodded. "It felt so real. Amanda was here. She held me and said to stop this vendetta. She told me to look after her niece," I said with a tiny smile, my hands roving over my tightening belly. Caressing my baby bump, I finally realised what was at stake; my baby girl! I'd lived through that fateful night; I'd already lost so much, but I'd also gained Kade and the baby. *Our* baby. This wonderful, unusual man was part of my tiny family unit. I couldn't jeopardise what I had, what *we* had. I had to look out for our daughter.

Kade interrupted my thoughts, "Dream or not; I think she's right, baby, it's too dangerous. Your health, mental and physical, comes first, and on that note, let's get you inside and into some dry clothes and warmed up."

He helped me from the car; arm wrapped tightly around my shoulders as he assisted me up the path in my heeled boots. Feeling lighter of heart than I had in an age, I snuggled closer into his body, realising I was falling in love with this beautiful being. Who would have believed the nightmare I'd endured would give me that special someone? One I could see spending the rest of my life with; and yet, my life would only be a drop in a rainstorm compared to his eternal presence in this world.

***

The scent of frying steak and onions permeated the house. I turned off the shower, quickly patting dry my pink and pruned skin, and followed my overly stimulated nostrils down to the kitchen. The smell of food had me salivating, hungry to tuck in.

The plate on the table was piled high with steak, onions and chips, and beside it, a bottle of tomato sauce ready for me to drown my chips in. Yum!

"Enjoy. Umm, is it okay if I grab a shower while you eat?" I nodded, unable to answer, my taste buds exploding like fireworks, as the juices trickled past them. Wow, this man could cook!

By the time he reappeared wearing those deliciously tight jeans and nothing else, he found me leaning back in my seat, sated. Arms hung languidly down my sides, head leant back against the wall, filled to exploding and so very, very tired.

"I need to move, or I'm gonna sleep right here," I said. "Fancy a coffee?" He nodded as he finished towel drying his hair.

Collecting the mugs from the dishwasher, I brewed the coffee, liberally adding sugar and cream to his mug as I'd seen him do, and then carried them through to the lounge.

Kade was at the stereo, thumbing through Dad's collection. Finding the vinyl I'd purchased for Father's Day last year, Beethoven Concertos, he slipped it from the sleeve and placed it on the turntable. Then flicking the switch on the heater, he sank down into the couch. Contentment enveloped me as we sipped at the sweet coffee and watched the faux flames in the firebox, allowing the music to swirl gently around us. Quietly, Kade began to talk.

"You know, I never tire of listening to Ludwig play; now he was one guy that should have become a vampire! Just imagine the magic he could compose today when his playing was super powerful three centuries ago." He paused, a thoughtful look across his face. "I suppose in his own way; he's already immortal, his music spanning so many lifetimes. I had the privilege to hear him play in Vienna."

I stared in shock. I knew Kade said he'd been around the block a few times, but this, this was, WOW. He was alive when Beethoven was composing. My God, he had seen it all, life evolving for three-hundred-plus years. What stories he could tell!

"Are you okay? You're staring at me like I've grown horns or something. I haven't, have I?" He asked with a sudden grin, his hand searching his forehead.

"No." I grinned back. "I was just thinking what a wonderful storyteller you'd make, or history teacher even."

"No, I don't think so. History books; which *claim* to be historical facts, is the history I'd be made to teach. It's fiction, claiming to be fact; when all they are is theories of the people who wrote them. Parts that are real are turned, twisted so much that the good, the bad and the downright despicable all read the same."

I thought about some of the books I'd studied at college and nodded, wondering how many of them had been altered to suit the course the author wanted it to take. A yawn crept up on me, and he chuckled.

"See, not such a good storyteller, I send my listeners off to sleep."

"So not true," I quickly disagreed. "I'm just so tired; I think the huge meal did me in."

"I'm just teasing, you go, and I'll clean up here and lock up. Oh, um." He stuttered as comprehension kicked in that he'd taken for granted that he could stay. "Sorry, I um …"

It was so comical; I smothered a giggle in the collar of my dressing gown.

"You wanna sleepover, Kade?" I asked a little tongue in cheek, positive that his face reddened a little, embarrassed. It was kind of cute.

"Sure," he answered, eyes twinkling at me. "I'll lock up, shall I?"

I laughed at him and nodded, turning toward the stairs as he collected the cups and disappeared through the kitchen door. Before I was even halfway up the stairwell, a whisper of movement told me he was right behind me. I shook my head softly. *What must it be like to possess such speed?*

Hand in hand, we gained the top of the stairs and headed to my room. There was no awkwardness between us this time as we discarded our clothes and slipped between the sheets. We made love to each other, hands touching, feeling, caressing. Soft, moist lips meeting over and over, tongues licking, sucking, tasting. Excitement building as we finally joined. There was no pain, no fear as we moved together seeking the climax that would lift us both high enough to reach the dark, cloudy night sky. Finally sated, we gently floated down, and within minutes, I was asleep, safe in his arms.

<u>**Chapter seventeen**</u>

A week passed in a blur, my stomach expanding daily. The only time Kade and I were apart was when he disappeared for a few hours, returning with eyes bright, green and sparkling, after quenching his thirst on some vampire junky.

We spent much of our days exploring each other, exhausting ourselves on our lovemaking and sleeping away the daylight hours when the sun held Kade a prisoner within the walls due to his highly sensitive eyes. Honestly, this was no hardship to either of us as we became lost in our own little world.

We did manage one day out; the wind whistled, and the dewy rain allowed for a lovely drive along the winding country roads, hedgerows high around us. Kade requested we visit the places closest to my heart.

We crept through the sleepy town of Beaminster and took the road to Netherbury. My Aunt and Uncle had lived their entire lives in this gorgeous little village.

Climbing from the car, we trudged across the heavily pitted soccer field, the earth punctured by the endless studded boots creating a paradise home for the pink and wriggling earthworms. Approaching one of the benches, I ran my hand reverently over the stained wood. My uncle had purchased the bench seat as a dedication to his wife. Her love for the game and her village team making this her special place. I barely remembered her, and yet whenever I was here, I felt at peace.

"My uncle's ashes were scattered here, right next to her bench," I told him.

Tears rolled down my cheeks at the gentle memories. *Had Dad been reunited with his long-lost sister? With my Mom? Were all my family together, without me?*

Blowing a kiss towards the bench, we left the field and climbed back in the car.

Kade listened intently as I regaled him with stories of my past as we drove through the places which held my memories. I described the market days held in Bridport, and how Dad would take Amanda and me on a Saturday morning outing, followed by a walk along the cliffs at the Bay, or a quiet afternoon fishing from the piers. The chilly day didn't stop me from opening my window as we fair flew along Station Road towards our next destination; Abbotsbury. The wind created a booming vacuum in the car. My hair streamed back, and tears streaked my face but, oh my, I felt so alive. We were heading to a very special place; the beach on which my dad proposed to my mother.

The view from the Abbotsbury hill always took my breath away.

"It's so beautiful, isn't it?" I gushed.

Kade nodded, he'd gone quiet a little while back, a frown marring his stunning good looks, deep in his thoughts, but my comments had him turning to me with a smile as he took one hand from the wheel and smoothed my hair back.

"Slow down, babe, we need to take a right along here," I warned as he indicated and swung into the bumpy lane.

The fine pebbles crunched underfoot as we made our way towards the breakers. This place; the air, the great expanse of open sea and the knowledge of my folks creating one of their happiest memories here, worked its magic on me. I felt my mind and body relax in a way it hadn't since I lost my family.

"We need to come back here with our daughter," Kade announced. "It's beautiful, and the serenity of the place works for you. You're content here."

"Crazy, huh? After all that's happened, I didn't think I'd ever be happy again. But this place, it's like the wind massages away my pain, the aches, the scars, and casts them out to the ocean." My cheeks heated as I heard the words slip past my lips. "Sorry," I said with a chuckle. "Sounds a bit corny."

"No, Dani, it's not corny if it's true. I mean, look at you, you're glowing."

Blushing, I cast around my head for a change of subject. "Hey, there's no one around, how about a demonstration of some of these superpowers of yours?" I put the suggestion out there, and in the blink of an eye, I was alone. *Where the hell?* I thought.

A loud whistle sounded, and I squinted along the stony beach, barely seeing the figure waving his arms at me. "No freakin' way." Next thing I knew, I was in his arms, and we became part of the wind as we blurred across the pebbles. Stopping suddenly, he put me down on shaky legs, keeping his arm around my shoulders as I bent to take in some deep gasping breaths. "Oh my god," I sputtered, "that, was mental."

He laughed at the shock on my face. "You did ask," he said as he nudged us forward and began the long walk back to the car. "Come on; we're about to get a drenching."

I looked at the darkening clouds and then wrapped my arms around his neck. "Okay, Superman, fly me back. It'll be much quicker."

***

Water dripped from our clothing, drenching the seats. He was fast, but not fast enough.

A while later, showered and dressed in leggings and a jumper, I waited for Kane to come down. When I caught sight of him, I was struck with an embarrassing case of the giggles as he sauntered into the kitchen barely wearing my father's old dressing gown, the length leaving little to the imagination.

"What?" he said, eyebrows wiggling comically. "There wasn't much to choose from since you stole my clothes."

"I didn't steal them." I chortled. "They're in the dryer. Maybe you should grab a bag of stuff next time you're out."

With a twinkle in those sexy green eyes, he dragged me from my chair, caught me up in his muscle-bound arms and kissed me senseless.

"I think that's a wonderful idea," he said as he released my lips, leaving me gasping for air.

Time disappeared as I sat entranced, listening to his many stories. Of course, with the numerous years he'd lived (can I say lived, when technically he'd died?) and experiences to share, it left little time for me to dwell on what to do about Jake's crew of misfits. Pushing them to the back of my mind, I chose to live instead for the moment, and cement our new relationship, learning more and more each time I fed on him. Every sip was a lesson in the lifetime of Kade. I began to eagerly look forward to the moment when I'd put my lips to his wrist and watch his story as I fed; flashing on his memories of war-time, imbibing on the blood from wounded and dying soldiers, watching as the pain in their eyes changed to a euphoric glaze, dying in peace. Kade became their angel of death, helping them in their hour of need as he delivered them from their pain-wracked bodies.

I held witness to him, dressed in period costume; so very sexy in his long coat and cravat, bending women in crinoline gowns, their bosoms exploding over the corseted top, over his arm as he sank his fangs into the slender, white columns of their neck. Jealousy, the green-eyed monster raised its head as I'd glanced down at my gaudy track pants and singlet.

One evening, basking in the afterglow of our lovemaking, my fingers gently tracing his ribcage, lower and lower to the V pointing beneath the blankets, I decided it was as good a time as any to ask the burning question.

"Can you remember what happened to you? When you were turned?" I asked.

My lips pressed tiny kisses over his chest. I didn't dare look up, didn't want to see his face in case the question was painful for him.

He lay silent for the longest moment, and as I opened my mouth to take back the query, he began to speak. "After my mother died, I felt there was nothing left. I buried her in the tiny cemetery on our church grounds. I wanted nothing more than to fling myself in with her." I nodded softly in agreement; I knew that feeling.

"They were hard times, Dani. Poverty, starvation and disease ran rampant among the people in our village, and every other village too, I suppose. My mother was barely cold in her grave when our home was stolen away by a couple of ruffians. They broke into the house while I was working in the fields, and when I returned and discovered the squatters, they beat me nearly to death and left me on the road to die. I wasn't that lucky. I survived on the streets, sleeping the warm nights in the fields and the cold ones in a nearby quarry. I ate what I could catch or pilfer, drank whatever liquor I could lay my hands on and didn't give a damn if I were to live or die."

He went silent for a while, remembering. I shivered, picturing what it had been like.

"Things changed when four strangers arrived in the village. There was a small inn, rooms which they procured, nothing like the hotels and resorts of today, this was a rough stone building, with the grand total of five rooms if memory serves me, but it was warm and dry, and food and ale were available for those who could afford it.

"The townsfolk watched the newcomers with more than a little suspicion. They were so different from anyone we'd seen before. They attracted quite the entourage; people followed every time they took to the street, myself included. They were always dressed in their dark flowing, hooded capes. They appeared to know the village well, walking the dirt roads with ease. I followed them the day they visited

Lina's hovel; hiding nearby, watching, trying to hear what they wanted from my father's old friend. From what I overheard, I determined they were a religious order, preaching words of 'forgiveness', and calling the old woman 'my child'. It seemed Lina was no stranger to them, which of course made the villagers even more uneasy. The fact that they spoke a different language between themselves and freely tossed coins to any beggar close by made them an interest and a target. Not only for people like me who could always do with a coin or two in my empty pockets, but also for the more mercenary of the villagers who would slit their throats as quick as look at you while stealing their bounty.

"An uproar broke out when a number of these vicious thieves were discovered several days' later; blood drained from their bodies. Nobody could prove the strangers had done it, and we probably wouldn't have condemned them if we had found proof."

I sat up, tucking my feet beneath me, entranced in his story.

"The night you're interested in, fell on All Hallows Eve, quite befitting the story really. In this century, it's all a good night out, monsters and ghouls partying in the streets. Not so back then; there weren't people out that night celebrating. The townsfolk shuttered their windows, stayed inside and kept their doors barred against all that was evil. It was widely known that All Hallows Eve was the night that the king of all evil rises, to pillage, rape and murder any who dare walk beneath the dark skies.

"As for me, I had no door to close and, like one of the spectres the villagers feared, I haunted the inn, begging for a coin to purchase a jug of ale to drown my sorrows, when the strangers appeared on the steps, speaking their strange language to one another.

"They moved swiftly through the quiet village, and I had the strongest urge to follow. I ran from building to building, keeping myself hidden in the shadows, struggling to maintain a visual.

"I was darting between two buildings when the younger of the two women turned and saw me. She looked to be younger than I; her long black hair fell like a waterfall to the middle of her back. Her eyes were so black that even in the darkness surrounding us, they gave me the shivers. She called something to her companions, and they all turned and stared. Their pale skin was waxen in the moonlight, and I noted that each possessed those same dark eyes that appeared to glow as they moved toward me.

"She questioned me, asked me why I wasn't afraid to be out that night. I remember her voice was musical, her accent making our native tongue almost pleasant to the ears. I told her I had no home, no abode, that I was out every night.

"When she suggested I walk with them, I did. I walked for what seemed like mere moments, until she took my arm, and I turned, realising the village was far, far behind us. I'd been in some trance-like state. From the moment her eyes captured mine, the aching sadness I lived with and the gnawing hunger in my belly evaporated. Stupidly, I hoped this would be the end to my loneliness, that these people would become my new family. We walked on, stopping once reaching the edge of the cliffs and there we sat, legs dangling over the precipice as we watched and listened to the ocean pound the rocks below us. The moon's reflection shimmered on the waves, hypnotic in its power.

"When she took my hand, I was surprised and excited. Her fingers walked from wrist to shoulder, tugging me towards her; raining kisses on my cheek before dropping lower to nuzzle into my neck. She stopped briefly when her lips touched the crystal around my throat, hesitated in her task and then proceeded to make me squirm with desire. Her teeth grazed my skin, her tongue snaking out, intimately lapping every graze. In all honesty, I was becoming more and more aroused.

"It wasn't till much later, when I met more of their kind, that I realised she'd transferred her pheromone to me in the scraping of her fangs. I was in ecstasy, the feeling of floating, flying high as if I'd imbibed an entire barrel of ale. I wanted to take her, make her mine, never to come down from this floating abyss. But as she sipped the life from my veins, savouring like a connoisseur does an expensive wine, my head spun, and the earth rushed to meet me. A loud drum beat a tattoo in my head. My own heartbeat, once loud and fast, changed tempo, becoming slow, sluggish. My throat so dry, I could scarcely draw breath. Through a misty haze, I watched her companions' one by one rise and vanish into the night until only she, and I remained. Satiated, she daintily touched a kerchief to her lips and then she too stood to take her leave. I lay back against the bracken, near to death. Beyond thought or caring.

"Why she didn't leave me to die, I still don't know.

"She knelt, hoisted my body to a sitting position; I was so weak she had to hold me in place, and then she scraped a long, pointed nail along her breast and held my face against it. She ordered me to drink as she cradled the back of my head. My parched throat ached in response to the order. I remember trying to look up, wanting to see her face, but she wouldn't allow it. Pulling the tangy aroma of blood into my nostrils, my throat ached again. Running my tongue along the wound, I lapped at the drops of blood, needing something to relieve the aching dryness, but it wasn't enough. I placed my lips to the wound and suckled. Her flavour was intoxicating; the liquid gold ran strong and fast down my parched throat. She commanded me to sleep then, and I felt myself rise, I was airborne, flying, falling to nothingness.

"I awoke alone, cold and hungry, inside a small cavern that I had no recollection of entering. I made my way to the entrance and stood staring, surprised and delighted. The moon still hung bright, brighter in fact than it had as I'd perched on the cliff edge. Searching the surrounding wall of rock for a pathway, I discovered there were no obvious escape routes from the cave. I didn't know how I'd gotten there, but the only way out was down. I began my descent, scrabbling to hold the rocky cliff-face, stones cutting, biting deeply into my hands, scratching my arms and face each time I slithered when my grip loosened. I was terrified! It was slow, painstaking work and I'd only gained a few metres when the rocks beneath my clenched toes crumbled, my feet dangled, and my fingernails tore as I attempted to save myself. I fell.

"From that height, I knew there was no way I would survive. The jagged rocks came ever closer. I remember holding my breath, waiting for impact, the agony of being shredded on the rock. I was going to die, and I realised I wasn't as ready to embrace death as I'd previously thought.

"The expected impact never came. I landed on that beach, on my feet, knees bent, and when I straightened up, I just stood, stunned, staring at the waves pounding onto the beach, the sea spray soaking my ripped shirt and pants, the salt stinging the open scrapes on my body.

"I walked along the beach until I found an animal's trail zigzagging to the top of the cliff and followed the path, climbing higher and higher, not even breaking a sweat as I finally reached the lip and hauled myself over onto the grassy verge.

"There was no sign of the girl or her companions, but as I inhaled, filling my lungs, I could smell the sweet, sweet scent which belonged to her. Faint, so very faint and I knew she was long gone from the area. Alone once again, I struck out along the path and headed back to the village."

Kade stopped speaking and looked across at me. I sat cross-legged, bedcovers pulled around my shoulders. He stared at me, trying to read my face, judging my reaction to his tale.

"I'm not sure you need to know the rest; it gets a little messy," he said.

"Please, Kade. I want to know everything. I've seen so many memories while feeding, and some of them are damn graphic, I can take this. Please, I want to know."

He sighed deeply and nodded.

"Once I arrived back in the village, I headed to the Inn, hoping to find the group of strangers. The safe landing on the beach still puzzled me, and I was eager to discover what had been done to me. Their rooms were empty, the sweet scent lingered in the rooms, but they were no longer there.

"I wandered aimlessly through the village. There was something wrong, off, my senses seemed heightened, the village looked different, felt different, and it was loud. So many sounds reverberated through my eardrums; snoring, ragged breathing of the old and ill, the sighs of lovers and the squalling cry of a baby, loud, so very loud. I covered my ears to shut it out, and my sense of smell kicked up a notch. I could count the occupants in each dwelling by the scent emanating from the walls and window shutters. I removed the press of my hands from my ears, and the cacophony hit me again. I sucked in a breath and held it, keeping the smells at bay as I concentrated on the sounds. A thumping of a hundred drums, none in time with another, as I pivoted on the spot trying to pinpoint what it was. Round and round I went, and then it dawned. Heartbeats! I was hearing the heartbeat of every single villager. Finally releasing the breath I'd been holding for many long minutes, I realised I hadn't *needed* to catch my breath, there had been none of that burning ache in my lungs, no need for air, and it was then I noticed that the one heartbeat I couldn't hear was my own.

"I held my breath, again and again, longer and longer, and finally, the truth sank in. I didn't need to breathe. I didn't pass out from oxygen starvation.

I was dead!

"My life was over, Dani. The girl, whose name I never knew, had taken my life, and yet there I was standing in the middle of the village feeling strong and healthy, my hearing and vision better than ever before.

"I'd heard scary stories as a child about beings that were neither dead nor alive—not demons nor ghosts—but figures that were unholy and abhorred, yet who held such fascination. These were bloodsucking murderers who bore the name, vampire.

"I found myself standing at the door of my parents' home, and as I forced my way inside, I found sleeping, the two men who had beaten and left me for dead. One lay in my dear departed mother's bed. Anger struck swiftly and with it came an unquenchable hunger. I saw red, and then *they* were red as I tore them both to pieces, feeding on their blood before I trudged to the quarry and disposed of their shredded corpses into the deep water at the bottom of the sliding stones.

"Returning home, I cleaned every crevice, removing all signs of the scum that had inhabited my sacred space. I lay resting on my own cot as the day came and went. The events which had befallen me swirled in my mind. Then as night ascended over the village, I made my decision. Sliding my hand up into the soot-filled chimney and finding the loose stone, I seized hold, pulled it free, dropping it to the firebox below and felt for the possessions I knew were hidden there. With my crystal already fastened around my neck and a couple of other childhood treasures in hand, I stood by the door saying a silent farewell to my father, my mother and to the person I had once been, and I walked away.

"My belly was full, well-fed. But my anger burned hot for the girl who had taken everything without permission. She took one life and handed me back another, then left me alone, more alone than I had been before, to roam the earth as a monstrous corpse. A dead thing who murdered to feed the constant hunger, a monster who would never belong, never know the touch of love or hear the cry of his child. I cried for all that was lost to me; tears tinged red from the blood of my many victims."

I reached out for him then, moved forward and placed my lips near his ear. "You have my love, Kade, and you will hear the cry of your child," I whispered as I took his hand and placed it gently on the curvy roundness of my pregnant stomach.

A soft sob escaped him and then his lips crashed on mine. My hands frantically clutched his shoulders, pulling him closer as I kissed him back. There was no gentleness from either one of us; our lovemaking was a hot, frenzied passion. He buried himself inside me, deep and deeper. As he came, hollering my name, he dismantled his internal barriers and liberated his heart from three hundred years of loneliness.

<u>**Chapter eighteen**</u>

Something woke me, and I bolted upright, clutching the blankets to my naked breasts, or at least I attempted to, something was anchoring the covers. "What the …" I said and then saw what held them down, sadly, a fully dressed Kade, leaning back on his elbows watching me with those sparkling green eyes.

"Good morning," I croaked, swallowing to moisten my vocal cords. "You're up early."

His eyebrows rose, and I knew he was about to say something embarrassing. "I was famished after I … ravished you." He laughed. "So, I went out to wet my whistle and stock the fridge for our wee girl you're carrying there. You're gonna have to feed again soon, Dani."

He was right. I was feeling tired and weak, not my usual energetic self on waking. This baby had drained any reserves I had left after the energy I'd used during our lovemaking last night. "Breakfast time, baby girl," I said, caressing my belly. Looking up, I caught Kade ogling my bared breasts. "Hey, the baby comes first." Snaring the blankets, I re-attempted to cover myself up.

Pretending to growl, he bent forward and pulled the covers down to my knees, his eyes following the downward movement of the sheets and grinning. "That's better." Raising his arm to his lips, I watched in fascination as his fangs appeared and he pierced the tough skin of his wrist.

Grasping his arm in both hands, I leant forward, anticipation making me sloppy as a couple of drops landed on my thigh. I lifted his offering to my lips and licked the wound before latching my teeth around the punctured skin and drank. It was becoming a second nature to feed. Once I got passed the grossness of what I was consuming, I found I enjoyed the feeling of strength returning to my body; and the slide shows, instead of frightening me, became a way for me to get to know my man a little better.

I drank what I needed and wiped my mouth clean with a tissue. "Did you guzzle down on a smoker? I asked, the scent of smoke invading my now-enhanced senses. Holding tight to his hand, I used the tissue on him, watching in amazement as I cleaned the stray drops away and witnessed up close, the wound closed before my eyes. I don't think I'd ever get used to seeing that.

Releasing his hand, I leapt from the bed, only to be caught and pinned back against the pillows. There was no mistaking what was on his mind as he brought his head down and our lips clashed. His tongue waltzed with mine as we shared the rich iron flavour of the blood still staining my tongue.

As much as my body craved his, this wasn't going to get me out of bed. I had things to do.

I gave him an almighty push, the surprise on his face as comical as the shock on my own as he flew across the room, barely managing to get his feet beneath him as he landed beside the window.

"Oh shit, Kade, I'm so sorry. Are you okay?" I mumbled into the hand shielding the smile on my face. He stalked from where he'd landed with a grin of his own.

"Did we forget what vampire blood does for you?" he asked.

"Oops," I said, giggling full out now.

Leaning over, he planted his lips on mine in a quick kiss and then, putting his hands up, walked backwards to the door.

By the time I had finished in the shower, smells of breakfast had wafted up the stairs, making me quickly throw on a t-shirt and jeans, only to discover my jeans wouldn't quite fasten around my fast-expanding waistline. I dug into the bottom of my drawer and came up with a pair of old worn track pants, the elastic limp from too many washes, drew them up over my belly and headed to the kitchen. It was a little difficult to believe after I'd just fed on blood, that the smell of bacon had me salivating, hungry again. Eating for two on such different diets, was crazy, but hey, needs must!

Doorstop-sized slabs of bread with rashers of bacon stacked within were piled on a plate right next to the elixir of life, for which I beelined. Grasping the cup, I inhaled the delicious aroma of coffee. Seriously, my diet was so much nicer than our daughters. I smiled at Kade, sitting across the table from me as I chewed my bacon butty and sipped at my drink. "You're very quiet, what's up?" I asked, folding my hands across my baby bump. Kade hadn't said a word throughout breakfast. He glanced toward the hall, and I saw a bulging overnight bag with a newspaper folded neatly on the top. Raising my eyebrows at him, I asked, "Is that your way of telling me you're moving in?"

"Please don't think I'm pushy, but being here these last two weeks with you have been amazing. I want to stay with you, be near to keep you safe, keep our daughter safe," he responded, but for some reason, his eyes strayed from mine.

"What's happened, Kade? What are you hiding from me?"

Running fingers through his already tousled hair, his eyes finally found mine. "Dani, the last two weeks getting to know you, spending our time talking, laughing … loving." He winced. "I feel like I've found my rightful place, and I don't want to waste another second without you. I know that sounds corny, but …" he faded off.

His eyes locked on mine. I could see the truth, hell I knew the truth because it was how I felt too. I'd initially wondered if he stayed for the baby's sake until I remembered how his mother's crystal had sung for him after the first time we made love.

"Corny or not, I want you to stay. I wish my dad were alive to meet you; I think he'd have liked you." I smiled before a frown marred my face. "One question, though, what makes you think I need to be kept safe? Have you heard something?"

"Breaking news in the paper there may interest you."

Bracing myself, I asked the burning question, "What's it say, babe? What's happened now?"

"Maybe you should just read it yourself," he said, collecting the paper and depositing it on the table.

Scanning the headlines, I waited for something to jump out and shock me. *'More Brexit Mayhem, Keychain Supermarkets Sold, Yeovil loses racing brothers, Jamie Oliver's New Foods,'* Nothing caught my interest. Looking to him with a puzzled expression, I shook my head. "Thinking I may need a clue here."

Kade leant across the table and jabbed his finger down on an article, the headline black and bold on the page.

Yeovil loses racing brothers

The photo attached showed a couple of tall men, hair slicked back, and smiles prominently on their faces holding a 'first place' cup. I didn't follow car racing, but I read on.

'An early-morning tragedy in Burton Bradstock saw the demise of the racing duo, Jayden Lee Jamison and brother Frank Ira Gregory Jamison. The two had been working to ready their new prototype for this year's race. Cause of the accident, speed. No other casualties.
The road should reopen later today.

My mind remained blank, not connecting the dots. I skimmed the passage again. Something about the names seemed familiar. Could it be that Jayden was actually Jay? But what was the connection with Frank? And then I saw it. Frank Ira Gregory. F.I.G! My eyes flew back to the photograph. Could they be the same men? Photographed in their tidy, clean driving suits, hair above the collar, fringes long but slicked back, oiled in place. Their faces pink, clean-shaven. The two I remember were a total contrast, hair lank and greasy down to their shoulders, one with a couple of days shadow on his cheeks and chin and the other a full beard. Staring at the pair, I recalled the eyes shining in the light of the headlamps, the excited, triumphant gaze I'd seen that night now looked back at me from the black and white pixilated picture. I shuddered.

"How could nobody at the pub identify them? They are famous race car drivers!" I whispered.

"Dani, you were up close and personal, you etched their images into your brain. And you didn't recognise them from the photo. Pub lighting plus the facial hair and the way they were dressed, they obviously went incognito, and it worked."

"Okay," I sighed. "You're right. I didn't pick them from the photos. Shit, we just drove down that road the other day. Wait," my eyes flicked up to his, "did you do this? Where were you last night, Kade?"

He looked so cute as he scrunched his nose up at me and raised his eyebrows.

"Okay, busted! I knew the warehouse was their workshop. I found it weeks ago, and I was going to show you after we'd seen Max, but things kind of got put on hold with the baby and your sister's warning."

"That's why you were quiet on our drive that day, you went all serious and put your foot down along the road. They were there, weren't they?"

"We were close, way closer than I wanted you to be. I didn't want you to pick up their scent and ruin our day. After I fed last night, I was heading towards home to grab some of my stuff, and I caught a whiff of them on the wind. I followed my nose and found them reversing the car from the building and loading it into a truck. I guess they were sneaking it off to the track or someplace private to test drive it. Night would be perfect for that, no one around to see them and copy their latest modifications. I didn't touch them, I swear. Frank had just dragged the rear door down and was about to climb into the cab, and all I did was stand in front of the truck."

"That's it? You just stood there? No fangs? No freaky eyes?" I asked, eyebrows raised.

He nodded and grinned. "Yes, alright, I was a little vamped. Frank freaked, ran screaming from the truck and climbed into the car Jay was waiting in. Then Jay looked over and saw me and his foot hit the metal, taking off at a rate of knots. I followed on foot, keeping to the fields, appearing here and there through the hedges like the bogeyman; best run I've had in a while. I wish I had a camera so you could have seen their faces, the fear on them, you would have loved it. I reckon they were fair shitting their pants. Anyway, I kept up with them to that little area outside The Anchor, where they slowed down to access the one lane, and their car just exploded. I watched them die before they hit that wall, Dani.

"This is the reason I need to be close to you and make sure you're safe. The brothers may be dead and gone and no longer pose a threat to you, but that explosion wasn't an accident. Someone killed them, and as much as I wanted them dead for what they did, it wasn't me!"

"So, you think someone else wanted them dead? Maybe a rival racer?"

"I needed to get back to the garage before the police decided to lock it down. So, I didn't call it in, but I heard a car approaching as I turned to run, I knew the driver would call the emergency services.

Back at the workshop, their scents hit me as soon as I entered the building. Daz and Joe had both been there; the scent was fresh."

"Yes, but they were friends, it would be expected that they would visit each other at their place of work." I was trying to piece it all together and found the aroma of the men at the garage not suspicious at all.

"As I returned to the scene, the fire engine screamed past. The crash site was well ablaze and get this, the car which I'd spotted earlier, was parked up with a man leaning on the bonnet just watching the fire. He belonged to one of those scents at the garage. Doesn't it seem a little coincidental that one of those goons just happened to be onsite before the news of the crash even hit the papers? I think he was out there, waiting, watching for the explosion."

Chapter nineteen

"Kade, I don't understand why you would think they would turn on each other. You and I would be the obvious targets as witnesses to their crimes. Why take out their friends?"

"I don't know. Maybe our sojourn to Bottoms Up put a cat among the pigeons. I have no doubt Max ran ranting and raving to the others, telling them you were alive and intimately involved with the demon. If we truly scared him, he could come undone, go to the police and turn them all in. They can't trust one another anymore to keep the rape and murder a secret. Fear of being caught and imprisoned will turn people against each other."

Shaking my head in disbelief, I raised my mug and took a huge swig of coffee, gagging when I realised it had gone stone cold and spat it back in the mug. I gathered my plate and poured the rest of my cold coffee down the sink and began loading the dishwasher.

Was it possible that I could be in danger? Was I on their hit list? How difficult would it be for them to find me? It wasn't like they could scent us out as we could them.

With my head spinning with unanswered questions, I leant against the bench, reaching for the clean mugs. Something happened that had all those questions and worries flying out of the window. My stomach lurched beneath the waistband of my track pants, and my hands flew to cradle my baby bump. I flinched with the force of that kick, the feeling strange, a little nauseating but oh so wonderful. Our daughter was moving within me, changing positions, her tiny foot pushing at me from the inside. Magical!

Kade started, instantly aware of my mood change. "What's happened?" he asked.

"Look," I whispered and pulled up my shirt, standing spellbound as we watched in amazement as the baby undulated beneath my skin.

"May I?" Kade asked, holding his hand out. I nodded. The cool touch of his palm on my stomach had the baby doing somersaults as if she knew who was holding her. Maybe she did, after all, she lived off his blood. I wondered if she was privy to his memories as I was?

The delight on his face equalled my own; it was one of those special moments made to remember. Taking hold of my shoulders, he pulled me to him for a lingering kiss then folded me close within his arms—well, as close as my belly, and a kicking baby would allow.

"I think the baby wants you to stay," I said with a smile. "We will both be safer if we are together." Smiling, he turned away and collected his bag.

"I'll move this out of the hallway, don't want you tripping over it." He glanced at the stairs and then back at me with a strange look on his face. "Um, can I put my gear in your room?" he asked.

I nodded and, in a blink, he was out of sight up the stairs. Almost trance-like, I moved back to the table, the newspaper still covering it like a table cloth. And as Kade made his way back down the steps, I spoke. "You need to take me to the crash site."

"Why," he asked. "What would that achieve, except maybe to put you in danger?"

"It was my curse, Kade. If this has happened because of me, I need to see it. I need to own it. I know you don't want me anywhere near any of them. Please understand, I have to do this."

After a quick visit to Amanda's room for a wardrobe change, Kade may have agreed to take me, but only in disguise, we were off, speeding along the country roads. Kade helped me from the car, and we slowly walked toward the police cordon. There were several people lined up, cameras whirring as they attempted to capture footage of the wreck. Kade's description was spot-on, the car was nothing but a burnt-out casing; the heat must have been pretty damn extreme. I couldn't suppress the shudder as I thought how terrifying it would be to perish this way. As much as I hated them, this was just too awful.

Closing my eyes to the carnage, I concentrated on the different smells hidden within the smoke-filled atmosphere. Thanks to my early-morning feeding from Kade, (the smoky smell which had permeated his clothing made perfect sense now), I discovered it was easy to separate the individual aromas; gagging a little as I tasted the scorched flesh at the back of my throat. I quickly filtered the numerous scents and catalogued them, the perfumes, aftershave, damp dog hair and muck-covered farmyard boots, until … there it was. Daz! He invaded my senses, along with the charred remains of the deceased. The cocktail of smells drifted, growing fainter as the morning breeze stirred them and sent them on their way.

"We need to investigate Daz, what he does for work, where he hangs. We need to keep him under surveillance. And when he comes for us, we'll be waiting," I whispered loud enough for only Kade's vampire hearing to pick up.

Taking another deep breath to confirm my find; my eyes widened in a look of dismay as a newer scent hit my nostrils. Joe, he'd been here too. Why hadn't I picked up on it earlier? It was strong, so much stronger than Daz's.

I nodded at Kade and turned quickly away, moving easily through the crowd as they parted, allowing the pregnant woman to pass unhindered. With my head down, I almost walked into a man standing behind the onlookers. A quick glance up and a softly spoken "sorry" was more than enough for my heart to seize. I was wrong! Joe hadn't been here last night … he was here right now.

Thank goodness for Kade and his overbearing safety precautions. The quick change of clothes from my sister's wardrobe had my appearance totally different. Gone was my long dark hair tucked securely beneath a short blonde bob wig, a pair of horn-rimmed glasses I'd used for reading at high school and an old grey duffel coat which had been my father's, covered me from neck to knee except for my very pregnant belly poking through.

"Shit," I whispered softly, and from the corner of my eye, I watched Kade lower his head, hunching his shoulders a little as he caught the warning in my quiet expletive and Joe's scent all in the same moment.

Chapter twenty

"Excuse me," I muttered as I pushed past Joe, grabbing Kade by the hand and towing him along behind me. Once clear, I stood beside the car waiting for Kade to unlock it, taking one last peek behind; I had to know if we'd been detected or not. Joe's eyes trailed over Kade's hunched form, almost as if he sensed a familiarity. A frown marred the cleanly shaved face. And yet when he turned those same beady eyes on me, there was nothing, no hint of recognition at all.

My heart thumped violently in my chest, breathing rapid, and my head began to swim. The scrumptious bacon breakfast I'd scoffed down was lying heavy and doing its damndest to come back up.

The panic attack hit hard, my brain conjuring those terrifying moments once more; Amanda with the men viciously riding her, and standing victorious as they watched their mates inflict more damage. Jake's face, so close as I was held down. "I can't breathe," I gasped, clutching my chest. Kade swung the door open and pushed me swiftly to the seat, my feet flat on the gravelly ground; my knees spread wide. Applying gentle pressure to my neck, he bent me forward and pushed my head as far forward as my growing belly would allow. He stood, shielding me from the watching crowd as he slowly massaged my back with one hand, the other was held close to my face.

"Breath slowly, Dani," he instructed, "in through your nose." Inhaling deeply, I caught the scent of blood; my eyes snapped open to discover two tiny pricks of blood on Kade's wrist as he held it before my face. Distraction, he was distracting me, and oh boy, what a way to accomplish that. My tongue darted out and lapped at the precious droplets before they could drip. I felt rather than saw the shudder run through his body and a breathy sigh escaped his lips from way above me. I tongued the open wounds once more and was rewarded with a quiet moan. Panic attack and location forgotten; all I wanted was to hear more of those breathy moans. Cupping his hand to my face, I sucked gently, feeling his elixir of life blanket my tongue.

"You're killing me here, babes!" I heard him chuckle from above. I let him go with a grin. Slowly sitting up, I enjoyed the view as my vision climbed; knees to thighs, pausing for a long moment at the tell-tale bulge in his jeans and then up, up over his chest and finally, our eyes clashed. The world around us didn't exist as I pushed away from my seat and into his arms, and our lips met.

Parting reluctantly, I took a step back, "We need to go," I said, catching sight of several people gawking our way.

Once in the car, I took some much-needed deep breaths. "That was unexpected," I said with a grin as we buckled up.

"What? Joe or the kiss?" Kade asked, smiling to himself.

"Both. Thanks for the help. I seriously couldn't breathe."

"Um, I think maybe I should be thanking you; I was enjoying that." He laughed out loud. "Maybe we should head home and finish what you started," he offered, his eyebrows raised suggestively. I nodded my agreement.

Turning the key, we headed towards Yeovil. The scenery crawled past as we drove along the narrow road. A blue Corolla appeared in the rear-view mirror, and although we were travelling at the speed limit, the car behind was fast approaching. Was he chasing us?

Kade watched the vehicle in the mirror, but he didn't alter his speed as the car drew closer and closer. A sharp bend in the road lay only metres ahead, and I waited, bracing myself for a shunt from behind, listening for the squeal of breaks as the car slowed, but neither came. The reckless driver swerved into the opposite lane passing close by Kade's window before wrenching his steering wheel sharply to the left, almost cutting us off as he pressed his foot even more firmly to the floor and motored away from us.

It was Joe!

I clung to the dashboard for dear life as Kade hit the breaks to prevent a collision and then as Joe pulled away Kade pushed a little further on the gas, and we sped up as he attempted to keep the vanishing car in sight.

"Raincheck on what we started, sweetheart. I think we need to see what this idiot is up to." I nodded slowly, with a disappointed sigh.

Chapter twenty-one (Joe)

The horrific scene at the crash site made Joe's stomach turn. He may have done some shitty things in his past, seen some crazy stuff, but this was way, way beyond anything he'd come across before. The stench! Oh God, that alone would haunt him. Like a ghost on the air, it invaded his body as he breathed, wrapping its heat and tendrils within his chest, choking, crawling around inside of him. He coughed and spat. How the hell had this happened? The brothers were fucking professionals; his friends knew how to drive. When he'd caught the radio news, he couldn't believe it.

Firstly, why would they be racing on a village street and at night? Secondly, what were they driving? The duo wouldn't be racing their prototype through country lanes; they would have loaded it into a truck and secretly run it through its paces on the racetrack. Something was off here. He had to see the wreck for himself.

He hadn't been at all surprised to see the masses of people, like vultures at a fresh kill, milling around as they rubbernecked the burnt-out vehicle from behind the police tape. Even the heavy clouds hadn't deterred them from venturing out to ogle the unsightly spectacle.

Forcing his way into the crowd, he stopped suddenly as the smell made him gag. Bending forward, he breathed through his jacket to tame the stench and to calm the acid pushing its way up from his stomach. Straightening, he attempted to peer over the shoulders of the people ahead of him. There was a young couple right at the front, her hands gripping the police cordon so tightly; must have been one of the crazed fans the brothers were always dealing with. The bloke she was with was tall, over six feet and built like the line-backers he had watched on telly. But there was something about this guy, the way he stood, protective, an arm wrapped around the girl's shoulders, clutching her tightly to his body as if daring anyone to come near. He seemed vaguely familiar. Maybe if he could see his face, he'd recognise him. He checked out the tiny woman in his arms; her blonde hair rippled a little as her head shifted side to side as if searching for something. She turned slightly, and he noticed her eyes were closed behind the horn-rimmed glasses she wore, her chest rising and falling as she inhaled. Poor thing, if she were feeling anything like he was, she would be trying to breathe through the thick cloak of smoke and trying to stop herself from vomiting. He sympathised as his own stomach roiled again, deep down wanting to puke up last night's meal. He watched her a moment longer and saw her hand descend to her heavily pregnant belly, fingers slowly caressing the swell. Hell, she must be mental! Fan or not, this was no place for a pregnant woman. As the crowd thinned, he could finally see what lay before them. The car was burnt white, the fire so hot it had stripped away all colour from the mangled, twisted metal. His friends would have had no chance, caught up in the burning inferno. There was very little left of the car; he could only imagine what the bodies would be like. It was surreal. His friends were gone.

He stared at the carnage in disbelief until the blonde woman turned and almost walked into him. Her face raised to his, and she froze briefly before lowering her gaze to chest height. He could feel the warmth of her breath as it rushed from her lips as she muttered "excuse me" and bullied her way past with her male friend in tow. The big guy had his head bowed, his face hidden, but that feeling of familiarity touched him again, and his eyes tracked them as they approached a car. The blonde glanced back in his direction and appeared to have some kind of attack as she keeled over in distress, her friend rushing to her aid. He turned away, not wishing to witness her vomit splattering the stones.

Joe turned once more to the horrific scene, pushing to the front of the crowd and surveying the burnt and smoking tangle of metal. He swallowed the bile that burned his throat and, turning away, climbed into his vehicle. He needed to see Daz and check-in with Max to be sure they were okay.

His thoughts unwittingly flew back to the woman holding a glowing blade as she put a curse on them all. Was this her doing? He sat in his car, head laid back against the rest and closed his eyes as he relived that night as he'd done so many times. He had never felt such a high, as he had that night. Not a drug inhaled, swallowed or injected had ever created such a reaction. The sensation of that young girl beneath him as he'd pushed his cock inside her was like nothing else. She was so tight, so innocent. Her screams of pain had pushed his pleasure threshold up and up so high; he was floating. He'd barely been able to hold himself back, hated that he had to wait his turn, but oh

God, it had been worth it as he ploughed and dumped his load deep inside.

The small dark-haired sister whom Jake had ruined would have made an amazing main meal after the appetiser her sister had been. Shit, he'd have loved to have a turn at that piece of flesh.

But that atrocity, the monster-demon-thing, had laid waste to their plans. Was this abomination, with its glowing eyes and vicious fangs what she had summoned? Max claimed he'd seen them both together again; maybe they should have believed him.

Joe put the car in gear and slammed his foot down on the accelerator. He sped down the narrow road, the thought that his other friends may be in danger spurred him to drive faster than the legal limit. He pushed his car as fast as it could go, pedal flat to the floor. One car way ahead of him seemed to crawl along at a snail's pace as he quickly caught up, and without lifting his foot, overtook the vehicle.

With the speed he was driving, he briefly recognised the occupants of the slow-moving car as the couple he'd been watching. Did they live near here then? An image of the tall, thick-built man flashed in his mind and, for a split second, fear clutched at him as he realised the bloke's build and the way he'd clutched his little blonde, pregnant woman was reminiscent to the way the demon had clutched the chick Jake had banged. *Stupid,* he thought and almost laughed at himself, as he shook the thoughts of that night from his head. No way would demon-boy be snuggling up to some little blonde, pregnant bitch.

Within minutes, rural gave way to urban, and he lifted his foot; wouldn't do to get himself a ticket. Entering along the main street, he continued straight, glancing left and right at the crazy people out in this chilly morning air, living life, oblivious to the fact that a demon could be loose in the area. He turned the car and drove along an old cobbled street, the ridiculously bumpy road thinning to become one lane before it hit a sharp turn into another side street, which almost doubled back on itself. He continued up the road past the high school and parked outside of an old two-up two-down. Slamming the car door, he strode through a gap between two posts where once upon a time a gate had hung. He thumped the front door, the peeling paint sharp on his fist, and peered through the grime-covered windows of the entranceway. He watched as Daz trudged slowly down the stairs, stared at him for a moment through the dirt and dust and then unbolted the door. Ushering Joe inside, Daz closed and relocked it.

"Hey, what's happening?" Daz asked with a yawn.

"You still sleepin' at this time of day?" Joe questioned.

"Yeah, didn't get much shut-eye last night, if ya know what I mean?" He raised his eyebrows and palmed his dick. "What's wrong with you? You look like you've seen a ghost."

"You've not caught up with the news then? Not seen the papers or anything?" Joe said, his voice coming out fast and squeaky.

"Calm yourself, man. No, I've not seen any news. Sit down, and just tell me what's bloody happening," Daz growled.

Pulling a grubby kitchen chair away from the rubbish-laden table, he pushed Joe none too gently into it before heading into the badly lit kitchenette and flicking the switch on the kettle.

"There's been an accident," Joe said on a rushed breath. "Jay and Fig, they're both dead. The car crashed and exploded; it's gone, all burnt."

Daz's hand stilled as he swilled a couple of mugs, the water sloshed over his hands and ricocheted off the dirty plates piled in the sink and splashed the front of his shirt.

"Shit," he said slowly. "So, the lads finally killed themselves in that death trap, huh?" he said as he switched off the tap and began drying the mugs on the stained tea towel. Filling the mugs with boiling water, he added a spoon of coffee and stirred it in before handing one to Joe.

"It's all over the news, in the papers, on the radio," Joe said, taking a swig of the black coffee and pulling a face.

"Guess the Jamison Mobile wasn't so infallible after all," Daz mused.

"I um, was wondering, ya know, if it was actually an accident."

"Why do you say that?" Daz queried.

"Well, I err, was thinking about Max and what he told us, ya know. Bout the girl and her demon. Don't ya think it's a bit of a coincidence that she reappears and then this happens? She did vow to kill us all." Daz took a sip of his coffee, swallowing it down with obvious enjoyment as he watched his mate.

"Have you talked to Max about this?" he asked before taking another swig and letting the boiling liquid purposely sit, scolding his tongue, before allowing it to trickle down his throat.

"No, I came straight here. I can't believe they're gone, especially in a road accident, not the way they're used to driving. It just doesn't seem possible. I went over, had to have a look. It was horrible," Joe said, calming himself down a little with some long steady breaths.

Daz stood. "Come on, let's go. If Max has heard the news, he will be as wigged as you are right now, especially if he's still convinced that he's being stalked by the little witch."

Joe took his cup and emptied the thick coffee over the plates turning the congealed food on them a disgusting black. "You need to do your dishes, man, this is a germ fest right here."

"You sound like my old lady; fuck off," came the reply as Daz grabbed a cap from the table and slammed it over his tousled, greasy hair.

"Have you seen Max? I've not been near him since, well, you know, the night he called us all in. I'm guessing he sobered up and decided to keep quiet since …" He gestured with his hands between the two of them. "Since we are still here and not locked up."

"Yeah, I saw him the following day; still crapping himself and swearing it was definitely them that he'd seen, but he appeared to have gotten his shit back together," Daz answered as he collected his jacket from the hook. "Come on. Is your car out front?"

Joe nodded to him and led the way from the house. Daz followed, not bothering to lock it; now he was no longer inside there was nothing to protect, nothing worth stealing here. They climbed into the vehicle. Neither one noticed the white car parked a little further down the lane; half pulled in behind an old oak as it geared up and slowly began to follow them.

***

"Max! Come on, let us in!" Daz yelled as he pounded on the door. The spotless windows were a complete contrast to his own place. He could see Max as he hesitantly shuffled down the hall towards the front door.

"What do you want?" he called through the glass.

"Ah come on, mate, we're just checking to make sure you're okay."

The thuds of the bolts being drawn and the sound of jangling chains as the safety glided along the slider could be heard, and then the door inched opened.

"Is this any way to greet your friends?" Daz shoved his way into the house and scanned the room, immaculate as always. Daz wondered how the hell Max had ever been part of their debauchery; he was so squeaky clean. Max followed his friend through to the lounge room, leaving Joe to close the door behind him.

"Heard the news?" Daz asked.

Max stared at him for a long moment before he answered. "I heard it. An accident they said."

He regarded the men, eyes unblinking until Daz dropped down and relaxed into the sofa, commenting, "Well the Jamison Mobile obviously wasn't as infallible as we all thought it would be." The Jamison Mobile was what the brothers had nicknamed their prototype. It was their baby, designed by them, built by them.

Max took a step back and plopped into his chair; his face was suddenly wary. "What? Wait, they were in the prototype?" he questioned. "But they would never take that out on the road; it was track testing only! I was there last week when they were discussing purchasing a truck in which to transport the car from the garage to the track for the test run. They would never take the risk of having it photographed by the paparazzi."

"Well, they obviously changed their minds, since it crashed into the wall in the village last night."

"No! Max is right," Joe piped up. "I saw the wreckage. It was their road rally car. Both cars are similarly shaped, but it was definitely the road car that crashed."

This time Daz's face paled. *Not the prototype! Then what had made the rally car explode?*

Joe glanced between the two men, realising he was the only one still standing and suddenly glad of it when the nagging suspicion he'd felt earlier had him tingling with apprehension.

When he'd told Daz the news, the other man hadn't seemed shocked at all, hadn't even asked questions, like which vehicle it was or where the crash occurred. Now he seemed shocked to discover it wasn't the prototype that had burnt. Why would he have assumed it would be? And if he hadn't seen the news, how did he know the car had hit a wall in a village? Did he have something to do with the accident? Joe's thoughts flew back to the last time he was at this house, and the words Daz had said flew back to haunt him. *"Then I guess we deal with him."*

Slowly backing towards the door, Joe said, "Hey, Daz, you okay for a ride home? I got places to be." The room was suddenly way too small; he couldn't breathe properly. He needed to be gone, now.

Daz nodded as Joe opened the door and slipped across the threshold, holding onto his panic as he gently closed the door. Then spinning on his heel, he sprinted down the pathway and swearing quietly, struggled to get the key in the lock. Damn door, come on, come on, he kept glancing toward the house expecting Daz to come chasing after him. Finally, with the door unlocked, he threw himself into the driver's seat, turning to nudge the lock into place before inserting the key in the ignition and heading towards home.

Chapter twenty-two

Sneaking a peek, I watched Joe's speedy departure from Max's house and wondered what the hell had happened in there. Kade was nowhere in sight, having slunk around the building so he could eavesdrop on their conversation. Before leaving the car, however, he'd leant across and pulled a lever on my seat, dropping the back down, so I was lying out of sight, left wondering what was happening. I couldn't help it. Too nosey to be left out entirely, I was up leaning on my elbow trying to capture a glimpse of Kade hiding somewhere in the shrubbery. I saw Joe slip from the house and then leg it to his car.

I shrieked when the driver's door was yanked open. I'd been so busy watching the house I hadn't noticed anyone approaching the car. Panic gripped me as I turned. Kade with a knowing smirk on his face slumped into the driver's seat. "I told you to stay down, not go peeking," he admonished me.

Catching my breath, I heaved myself into a sitting position and thumped his arm. "You trying to make me go into early labour or something? You scared the bejesus out of me."

He chuckled and leaned across behind me as he readjusted my seat.

"So, what did you hear?" I asked, wanting to know word for word what I'd missed. I listened intently as Kade repeated what had been said.

"I'm wondering if Daz wasn't the culprit after all. I know we had his scent at the crash site, but listening to him just now, that was genuine shock in his voice. We know he witnessed the flaming car, but obviously, with the smoke and fire, he hadn't identified which vehicle it was. As for Joe, I think he may have clicked to the same conclusion to have him legging it out of here. Max, on the other hand, seemed strangely calm. Nothing like the last time we saw him. I wonder if he's the one who staged the accident after all?" Kade pondered out loud.

"Surely not. You never mentioned scenting him at the garage, so, how could he set a device?" I questioned.

"He said he was there with the brothers when they were discussing buying that truck; they could have been at the track or a pub, anywhere. I would dearly love to check out this prototype though, see if I can find anything planted on it."

"The cops will have it in lockdown, surely," I said as I fidgeted with the seatbelt as it pulled uncomfortably tight across my swollen abdomen. Realising I still wore my disguise, I tugged the blonde wig off, throwing it into the back seat and massaging the itchy heat of my scalp. Silence enveloped us as the scenery flew by.

The click, click, click of the indicator woke me with a start; I hadn't realised I'd even closed my eyes. Sleep seemed to sneak up on me a lot lately. All part of this pregnancy lark, I guessed. A quick glance around had me sitting straight up; I didn't recognise where we were. The car seat jolted like it was atop a pogo stick, over a pot-holed country track. "Um, where are we?" I asked.

"I want you to meet someone," he said and offered nothing more in the way of explanation.

As I squinted into the distance, an old manor house came into view. It looked empty, uninviting. There was no smoke trickling from any of the numerous chimneys, which was odd considering the day was cold, cloudy and damp. The yards and paddocks surrounding the place were deserted, not a sheep or cow in the fields, not a single chicken in the chook house, and once the engine noise died away, the silence was deafening and frightening.

As empty as the place appeared, it was not decrepit in the least. The gardens were well-tended, and the paintwork on the house wasn't peeling, or lichen-covered as one would expect of a deserted property. I looked to Kade, eyebrows raised, silently questioning.

Exiting the car, I couldn't help but shiver a little, partly from cold but mostly from fear. There was something *off* here.

"What is this place?" I whispered, fearful of breaking the heavy silence.

"It belongs to a very old friend. Someone, I think you need to meet," he added cryptically.

Mounting the steps leading to the enormous entryway, he flipped the huge handle downwards and pushed the heavily panelled door wide open. *Just how good of a friend was this person?* I thought.

Stepping aside, he motioned me forward, and I tentatively stepped over the threshold. Kade followed close behind and quietly closed the door.

The inside was huge! Closed doors to the left and right, which would have long ago housed cloakrooms and a place for the doorman to hide away out of sight. A long high-ceilinged lobby was skirted on both sides by flowing staircases coming to meet in the centre, forming a viewing balcony, stunning, romantic; I envisioned ladies in their crinoline gowns waiting patiently, watching as the guests entered, hoping for a secret lover to arrive. I shook my head. This place was playing with my mind.

The décor was old school, well maintained, and I imagined the main structure remained unaltered from when it housed its original lord and lady.

My mind took flight, like a scene in a book, of tattered tenants, with cap in hand, bowing low as their hard-earned coins were passed to the landlord. Oh, the memories this old manor must hold.

Fresh flowers adorned each alcove in the walls, and large arrangements in ornamental, twisted glass vases were placed on the two tables on either side of the door. The abundance of blooms creating colour and warmth, the perfume sweet and welcoming, although the house itself was chilly, and I pulled my coat as far across my belly as I could as a shiver travelled through me.

Kade patiently stood, allowing me to peruse the surroundings and then gently took my elbow and led me towards the closed doors directly below the balcony. Once again, walking in uninvited. Maybe he had contacted his friend before we came?

"I bid you welcome, Kade. So many years between visits. I was sure you had forgotten me," a feminine voice came from the direction of the armchair facing the window. I glanced uneasily around; this was a drawing-room; almost like being inside an old television programme, I almost expected to see the suave Mr Darcy riding his horse across the manor grounds just like the opening take of Pride and Prejudice, one of my favourite series as it happens. I mean, Colin Firth in those britches, who wouldn't be watching? But there was no horse and rider coming across these open empty fields. What could she be watching out there?

"Julianna, my dear, dear friend, as if anyone could ever forget you," Kade cooed, approaching the chair and tugging me along with him. "I have someone very special to introduce."

Reluctantly allowing him to manoeuvre me to the side of her chair, I was struck speechless as the woman uncurled from her seat, stood and faced me. She was breathtaking. Face to face, I realised we were the same height, and yet this tiny five-foot-two temptress exuded a personality one hundred times the size of her petite form. Her face alone could stop a war or start one. Beauty beyond compare was this tiny goddess amongst us.

I fought the temptation to bow down, to curtsy at the introduction. I settled with a slight bob of my head as I scanned this piece of perfection. White-blonde hair twisted and pinned with loose ringlets hanging gently past shell-like ears, the tendrils long enough to caress the flawless skin of her shoulders. Her long, slender neck was adorned with an amethyst worry stone which hung from a long golden chain. Long, amethyst-tipped fingers, moved back and forth, caressing the worn crystal.

Ample breasts played peek-a-boo from the top of her purple, velveteen gown and her impossibly tiny waist was cinched in, accentuating the lush swell of her hips. Not one blemish marred the white porcelain of her skin. Lilac-coloured makeup painted her lids and lips, the latter tilting upwards at the corners as if she were laughing at some private joke. A smile, and a flash of small white teeth as her tongue darted out to moisten those lilac lips, making them shine. Wrenching my gaze up and away from those luscious lips, I watched her eyebrows lift in a fine arch, and below them, glittering aquamarine eyes studied me. Inhaling, tasting my scent, her eyes slowly changed, the marine green vanished. Dark blue, navy, and then hungry black eyes challenged me.

'Run,' I thought I heard, although her lips never moved, and then that tongue flicked again, and I was already turning to make my getaway.

"K-Kade?" I stammered my heart hammering in my chest as I took my first step. His arm reached out, wrapped around me, and I stilled.

"It's okay, Dani," he whispered and turned to the vampire. "Julianna, meet Dani, *my girlfriend,*" he verified. "Dani, this is Julianna."

Black eyes scrutinised the protective way Kade's arms held me. I bravely held my ground as she stepped towards us, leant and took a deep breath. Her nostrils quivered slightly before her brows dipped into an unbecoming frown.

I held my hand out to her; very proud of myself when I noticed only a faint quiver in my outstretched hand. "Pleasure to meet you, Julianna," I said quietly.

She continued stroking her worry stone with one hand but brought her other down and laid it in mine. I shivered at her touch; the hand was so very, very cold.

"Dani, I welcome you. Apologies, I did not mean to frighten you."

The grip on my hand was firm yet gentle as she drew me closer. Kade released me as I willingly moved to stand within her personal space. She lifted both arms and laying those manicured fingers on my shoulders, turned me like a spinning top. "She has not been marked! Kade, you've not sampled this delightful creature. You have come needing my assistance, yes?" she asked.

"Yes." Kade nodded.

Her fingers stroked my neck, as they had her worry stone, back and forth, and my breathing hitched. "Do not be afraid, Dani," she said, raising my hand to her face. I watched in horrified fascination as those tiny white teeth morphed; two sharp incisors appeared as if from nowhere, and I panicked, attempting to wrench my hand free. I was like a moth, frantically fluttering, trying to escape from human fingers which so easily held me captive. But this was no human, and I was no moth. "Calm your woman, Kade!"

His arms instantly surrounded, caging me as he whispered in my ear. "She will not harm you, don't be frightened. It is a simple tasting, the vampire equivalent to a blood test at your doctors, nothing more."

Easy for him to say. "Doctors use needles, not fangs," I whimpered.

"Trust me, sweetheart. She can help us." His lips caressed my ear, his breath warming, and I closed my eyes and relaxed against his chest. I trusted him to keep us safe.

A tiny pressure, as he said, nothing more than a needle prick, and my eyes opened as Julianna's tongue swept across the tiny red droplets. Her eyes closed, and a look of pain crept across her features. Her lips parted and, like a child with a lollipop, she took my digit between her lips and sucked, whimpering as my life-giving fluid waltzed across her tongue, tantalising her taste buds. She swallowed and released me from those lilac lips. Her eyes snapped open, her pupils dilating as she studied me. I was nothing more than a piece of flesh pressed between two slides under a microscope. Her eyes noted everything as her tongue danced once more across my finger, and I watched in surprise as the miniature puncture vanished without a trace.

"Well, well, who's been a naughty little vampire then? What have you been up to with this little human, Kade? You are all through her. I taste your scent on her body and your blood pumps in her veins. You are feeding her, messing with my reading! This goes against our rules … unless…" She stopped and glanced down at my bulging middle.

Embarrassment coloured my face as images of the intimacy Kade and I now shared flittered through my mind, and wanton heat filled my body. Tugging my hand from hers, I could only hope she hadn't noticed the sudden warmth flow through my body.

"The child she carries requires my blood to survive," he answered her unasked query. His arms relaxed and, instead of holding me in place, they now draped over my shoulders. Leaning lightly atop my breasts, his hands caressed the top of my belly and our daughter beneath.

"The child is like us?" she asked.

"She is half-human, half-vampire," Kade responded.

"How?" she inquired. "How is it she knows of our kind? How did she conceive this hybrid? She would have required your blood at the same time as she was …" Her eyes widened, and her brows arched. "Juicier and juicier. Are you into threesomes these days, Kade? Or were you being heroic, offering her your blood to save the poor maid's life?"

"Poor maid!" Kade chuckled. "She bit me," he said, and I could feel his chest vibrate against my back as he laughed. "Just sank her teeth into me, swallowed my blood; saw a heap of my memories and …." His words ran out at the look the other woman was giving him. "Aww, come on, Julianna, I know what you're thinking, and I couldn't do it."

I was following the conversation just fine until then. I stared at her, trying to read in her expression what Kade had seen. What was going on in her head?

Oh! She was wondering why he hadn't killed me there and then to keep their secret. Funny really, since I'd asked him the exact same question.

"Why?" The question fell from her lips.

"She told me not to," he whispered and bent to place his lips to the top of my head. "She's mine, I found her. Dani is my soulmate!"

"Soulmate!" Her voice rose. "After three hundred years of searching, you finally found your soulmate, and she bit you?" Her mouth opened wide as she let out a very unladylike guffaw. The laughter warmed her eyes, and they turned back from black to aquamarine in a flicker. The vibration against my back became more of a shake as Kade let go of his mirth and laughed alongside her.

I stood as the beautiful people laughed together, at my expense I might add. Finally, the laughter turned to chuckles and then a comfortable silence as she once again grasped my fingers and led me over to the couch.

"I'm sorry, Dani, I have no refreshments to offer you. I do not entertain humans in my home." And once said, she seemingly floated back to her chair. Kade took the seat beside me, his arm hanging loosely across my shoulders. I still wanted to know what help he needed from this petite woman. I didn't have to wait for long.

Sitting in the room with not one, but two vampires should have probably weirded me out more than it did. Strangely, I wasn't uncomfortable in her presence, now that her eyes had changed back, and her fangs were hidden from view.

I was happy to cuddle into him and listen to their conversation as she questioned him about the hows and the when. Her gaze strayed often to my stomach. I could feel the gentle movement of my baby as she moved restlessly, the fluttering making me smile.

Suddenly, Julianna's hand was on my abdomen. I gasped and let out a tiny squeak. I hadn't seen her move. One moment she was in her chair and the next kneeling on the burgundy rug near my feet, her eyes on my face. The burgundy rug pulled my gaze, the colour so vibrant in this cold room. *Burgundy: hmm, I wonder if that rug hides blood well?* Shaking my head, I brought my thoughts back to the woman staring at me and holding my daughter beneath her palm.

The baby squirmed and kicked harder, and I gasped again, this time in pain as her little feet caught just under my rib. She was so strong; I truly believed my insides to be bruised black and purple.

"The assistance Kade has come for, is not for himself, Dani. It is for you and your child. I have delivered many, many children throughout my years. One was like yours."

I thought back. Kade had told me he knew of two other hybrids, and this woman had helped one of them into the world. No wonder Kade had turned to her for guidance.

The baby continued to kick viciously at Julianna's hands. "Enough," I said, pushing her hands from my body. "You're upsetting her." Instantly, the baby calmed, back to her usual fluttering again. It was as if my daughter felt danger, making me wonder if I was as safe with Julianna as Kade seemed to think.

Her eyes bore into mine for a long moment, probing, trying to read my thoughts but finally turned away. "Call me when the time comes, I will bring the powders for her to drink. Kade, help her to discover her comfort zone and teach her to concentrate on it. She may need it," she said cryptically before curling herself, like a cat, back into her seat.

Kade helped me to my feet before stooping over and placing a chaste kiss of farewell on her porcelain cheek. She never moved a muscle. "Come," he said and escorted me to the door. In the entranceway once more, I began to breathe a little easier. I had so many questions for him! But I held my tongue, knowing I couldn't ask anything until the manor house was far behind us and we were out of earshot of the tiny, but slightly crazy vampire within. Only when I was safely ensconced in the car, belted up and the heater blowing warm on my chilled feet did I dare to glance back at the towering manor, the grey, dreary, mist blanketed the old building. A movement in the second-floor window caught my eye. A quick flash, nothing more, and I knew Julianna watched us leave.

Chapter twenty-three

"I have questions," I piped up as we bounced along the potholed lane.

"Thought you might," he replied, taking his eyes from the track to grin at me.

"Stop grinning, this is so not funny," I responded. His face turned sheepish.

"Sorry sweetheart, I know it's not funny. Ask away."

"Do you trust her?"

"No," he answered, his face suddenly serious. "Julianna has lived in the manor for as long as I've known her. She is a recluse of her own making, leaving the mansion rarely. I wouldn't have taken you to meet her if I thought there was any danger to you or the baby, but, saying that, I would never leave you alone with her, Dani. You saw her reaction to your blood; she's lived on bagged blood and her deliveryman for years. Leaving you alone with her would be tempting fate."

I shuddered and wondered if the deliveryman enjoyed delivering more than just packages to the porcelain princess? Was he a vampire junky, needing his pheromone fix as she fed on him? Did he even remember, or did she wipe his memory of what she did, leaving his body burning with just enough temptation to feed his *need*, to keep him craving more so he would return repeatedly?

"How can you willingly place both our daughter and me in her care if you don't trust her?" *What was he thinking?*

"There's no choice, Dani. She's the only vampire I know with midwifery skills. We need her! It's not like we can have a human midwife and deliver her in a hospital. I'm thinking of the safety of those around us as well as you and the baby." He sighed in exasperation and quieted his voice with an effort. "Dani, think about it! A human cannot deliver a vampire child. We don't know what the baby's reaction to the outside world will be. What if she were to bite? Every baby born, human or otherwise, their first instinct is to feed.

"This miraculous child has taken a quarter of the time it takes a human foetus to reach this point. We can't risk exposing her to humans. I promise I won't leave you alone with Julianna. I will protect you and the child. Hell, we can set a safety circle if you want, keep your crystals close, and whatever you do, once the child is born, do not look Julianna in the eyes. The child will draw my blood from you as she's delivered, and you will be susceptible to mind control." He shook his head, exasperated. "I wish we had a choice in this, but she's the only person I know who can safely bring our baby into this world."

I choked back the rising sob before it could be released. I had to think of others as he was doing. He was right! I hadn't thought about what our child would be like when she arrived, hadn't considered the possibility that she could look or act differently to any other infant. My stomach flip-flopped as fear gripped me. What if she was a monster? He wanted no human near her when she was born, but *I'm* human. What if she tried to kill me? The baby squirmed as if sensing my fear, and I glanced down at the stretched pants hiding my ever-increasing mound. The sob that I swallowed fought its way back up, and I found my tears brimming as I watched the small movement of my daughter's hand as she gently stroked back and forth against the inner wall of my belly, soothing me, trying to convey that I had nothing to fear from her. She wouldn't hurt me. My fingers splayed over the movement, and I felt her hand push against mine. The tears trickled down my cheeks as I sobbed with relief, waving Kade on as I saw him turn to me and flick on the indicator.

We arrived home, and he ushered me quickly inside, closing the door on the misty darkness of the oncoming night.

The kitchen was a welcome sight. I hadn't realised how hungry I was. We worked like a well-oiled machine putting together steak and beans, the silence between us comfortable. Quicker than I expected, I was sitting at the table, fair shovelling the food into my mouth. Kade made coffee and sat opposite as he nursed his mug and watched in satisfaction as I finished my plate and mopped up the juices with a thick slab of bread. Swiping a napkin across my mouth, I settled back in my seat with a huge sigh. Now I was ready to talk.

"Julianna mentioned a powder, what is that?" I asked as I stirred sugar into my coffee.

"It's a relaxant, totally natural," he added quickly as he saw me about to object. "It's made from the flowers of a tropical plant which Julianna grows. The heating for the manor is directed into the conservatory to aid their growth since she doesn't need it. Vampires don't feel cold. The plants she grows have medicinal properties, safely used for centuries. The flowers you saw adorning the house are all grown on-site. The deliveryman I mentioned, collects the finished product, which is then sold on her behalf at various health stores. I can assure you, they are safe, for you and the baby."

Nodding, I cupped my hands, warming them around the mug as I inhaled the dark, swirling liquid and took a drink, taking my time to catalogue what he'd just divulged. Another sip and I pondered how to word my next question. "You said, you knew of two other pregnancies like mine, and I quote, 'both times the child was born healthy' but being born healthy doesn't imply that they lived …" I stopped, unable to continue, the fear of his answer silencing me.

"Sweetheart, have you been worrying if they lived or not?" he said, his puzzled look changing to one of concern. "You only had to ask. Yes, yes, they lived." I swallowed hard, and his scrutinising eye caught the movement. "What, what do you need to ask?"

"You say they lived?" He nodded his confirmation. "In what capacity? Lived like me or lived like you?" I finally choked out.

He was silent for the longest moment, and I had my answer.

"They were born vampires, weren't they? Not human." My voice quivered, and my brain immediately began searching for ways in which I, a mundane human being with a short life span, could parent a vampire child.

"No. Both were born and lived a human life … for a while," he said, setting his mug down and nervously tapping his fingers on the underside of the table. "But things happen, and neither retained their humanity, choosing instead to become full vampire," he finished.

"How long were they human, and who changed them?" The very question froze on my lips as the icy hand of fear gripped me. The thought of someone sucking the humanity from my daughter didn't bear thinking about.

"Raoul was thirty-six in hybrid years when he became non-human, and Jerome twenty-four. And they changed themselves; nobody forced them," he answered.

"Why? I don't understand. Why would they choose to become vampires?"

Kade continued to tap the table as if unsure how to continue. "Raoul's change was accidental. He got into a fight, a bar brawl over a woman, and Jerome just decided it was time; he didn't want to spend his immortal life looking like an old man."

"I don't understand. What does a fight over a woman have to do with him changing?"

"His temper got the better of him, he fought, the man bled, and Raoul tasted his first drop of human blood and couldn't control the bloodlust that comes with that first hit. He killed the man. Killing another human destroys the human side of a hybrid. As for Jerome, he woke up and realised he was ageing too quickly; he thought the only way to stay young, was to change."

"So, he murdered someone in cold blood because the selfish bastard was too vain to show a few wrinkles? He killed to stay looking young. Oh my god, how can any of you condone that?"

"Dani, it wasn't like that. He was a good man. He volunteered at a hospice, that's the place for terminally ill patients. Those patients never come out alive. He was so young, yet he was ageing daily, people were noticing. So, Jerome sought out the person in the most pain. The man begged for release, but euthanasia is still illegal. Jerome assisted him to pass with some dignity. He may have taken his life, but he did so by taking the mans pain, as an end to his suffering. It wasn't a selfish act; it was giving, caring."

"Oh." What else could I say? Again, I'd jumped to conclusions without knowing the full story. Would I ever learn?

Feeling slightly ashamed, I stared silently at the floor, going over all he'd just said. "What do you mean he was ageing too fast? You said he was twenty-four, that's not old!"

"I said in hybrid years, Dani, not human. That's one of the things which Julianna wants me to prepare you for." He reached out and took my hand. "The speed of growth doesn't stop when the baby is delivered. It's taken her mere weeks to reach full term, unlike a human child's nine-month gestation. Once she's born, her mind and body mature even faster than when in utero."

"How fast, Kade? How old was Jerome in human years?" My voice hitched as panic took hold.

Kade gripped my hand tighter, and with that tiny tell, I knew what he was about to divulge was bad. "Jerome was just closing in on ten months," he responded quietly.

No, this is impossible.

Disbelief clouded my mind. There was no way. He had to be mistaken. Please let him be wrong. This child, she was never meant to be! My daughter wasn't ever going to be a baby. I'd never have the chance to ween her to a bottle, diaper and cuddle her close like a normal child. I was to be denied the years of nurturing, of teaching her right from wrong.

Shaking my head side-to-side, I clasped a hand across my mouth to stop the screams as panic reared, and the realisation finally hit me — this child WASN'T HUMAN. Sigourney Weaver slipped through my mind, impregnated by an Alien; a sob escaped as my chest heaved, breath after ragged breath dragged in. Oh my god, I was just a vessel, a giant petri dish in which to grow an enzyme. Would this hybrid even require a mother? And besides that, she would be old enough to pass as my sister within a year, my mother or grandmother in two! I would watch her grow old.

I was hyperventilating, breathing out of control. Kade's hands grasped my shoulders, fingers biting, bruising the soft flesh as he shook me. "Breath slowly, Dani," he ordered. "In and out, breathe deeper, baby, come on." I took in a long shaky breath and huffed it out. "Again!" he said as I complied. "I'm sorry, baby, but you had to know. I know it's a lot to come to terms with, but remember, she's your child, and I promise you, she will love you, no matter her age. We will take every precious moment, and we'll make it count, whether she remains human or not. We can take photographs and commit every special moment to memory. She will be our baby, child, teen and adult, sweetheart, and you and I will love her. She is our very own special creation." Pulling me from the chair, he cocooned me within his arms, slowly massaging the stressed knots from my back and shoulders as the panic attack began to subside.

He was right! She would be special. She *was* special, and no matter what happened, she was my daughter, and I would love her.

Back under firm control once more, I whispered a heartfelt "thank you," and then stepped away, instantly missing the connection, but I still had one more question for him. "Back at the manor, Julianna said something about a comfort zone. What does that mean exactly?"

"To find your comfort zone is all about your headspace. Not a place, like a room or a beach, but that special place in your mind where you go when you're frightened or feel uneasy. Think back, when you were a child and woke from a nightmare, what did you do? What did you think about? Where was that safe place where the hurt or the monsters couldn't reach you? That was what she meant, a place in your mind that you feel happy and safe, a place to hide and gather strength if the pain or fear of birthing this child overwhelms you."

I frowned, trying to think back to a time when I had nightmares beyond my day-to-day existence. Before the rape. Before the deaths of my family members. Nothing! It was blank. I came up totally empty, and my face must have mirrored the dismay I was feeling.

"Why? Why do I need a place to hide? How different will this birth be? Is something bad going to happen?"

"Sweetheart, you just had a full-blown panic attack, your mind got away on you. Instead of following those threads that threaten you, go to your comfort zone, let it calm you. A calm mind will help you through labour and anything that follows."

"And if I can't find one?" He simply cuddled me close but didn't answer.

"Come on, love," he said instead, and he kissed the top of my head, walking us towards the stairs. "I'm going to run you a warm bath and then tuck you into bed. It's been a very long and emotional day."

Leaving me in my bedroom, he ventured into the bathroom, and within moments the sound of water rushing into the tub could be heard. Steam billowed from the open door which urged me to slowly shed my clothes and reach for my dressing gown. Sitting before the mirror, I gathered my long dark hair and, with a quick twist, pinned it into a bun. It had gotten so long, and I hadn't the energy to dry it tonight. I felt heavy, slow, and so weary as I shuffled my way into the bathroom. Kade turned the faucet off, then moved over to help me disrobe. He held my hand to assist me over the edge of the tub, helping as I carefully sank into the warm, caressing water and leant back against the bath pillow. Willing my shoulders to relax, I let out a deep sigh.

Half an hour later, I was dragged from the edge of oblivion by two strong arms sliding beneath my shoulders and knees as Kade lifted me effortlessly from the now-tepid water and carried me from the bathroom. Snuggling my face to his chest, one arm creeping up to the curve of his shoulder, my lids fluttered as I tried to stay awake, the fatigue from the day overpowering them. As I breathed his masculine scent, I relaxed, surrendering myself to the comfort he created whenever I was with him. I smiled, this was it, I'd found it. My comfort zone; my safe place! It was Kade.

<u>Chapter twenty-four</u> (Kade)

Kade watched from the doorway of the bathroom as Dani undressed and slid into her old dressing gown. He was worried about her; sad that she couldn't seem to find even one happy memory into which she could retreat if the need arose.

The steam from the bath he was drawing, drifted like smoke past him, but he couldn't take his eyes from the woman now sitting wearily at her dressing table. Her hands lifted her thick dark hair off her shoulders, and his gut tightened as the slender column of her throat was reflected in the glass, and the flawless white skin on the back of her neck was exposed to him as she pinned the hair high on her head.

He wanted nothing more at that moment than to kiss away her pain, little nibbling kisses across that soft pale skin. He had fantasised about sinking his fangs into that pale silken skin, and as she held her hair away from her neck, he felt himself harden, wanting her. To be in her, to taste her; to let her experience the pleasure of his bite as they made love; she knew of the aphrodisiac properties of his bite, and yet never requested he share the experience with her. Until she gave her permission, he would rein in his need.

He loved her. He had time; but did she? It was difficult watching as her poor human body painfully adjusted to her pregnant state. Humans weren't equipped to deal with the speed which a hybrid grew. Where other women gently caress, soothing their swelling baby bumps, connecting with their unborn child, Dani's hands didn't caress, they massaged, attempting to ease the pain, spreading lotion across the blue-veined, paper-thin skin. Mentally, she must be in hell; the loss of her family, the situation in which she fell pregnant, and then, the hardest of all, trying to comprehend that her daughter wasn't completely human.

Yes, he worried for her and himself. Three hundred years he'd searched for his soulmate. How could he cope if he lost her?

Sighing, he turned away, adjusting himself in his jeans as he went back into the bathroom to turn off the water. Dani entered the steam-filled room and dropped her robe. With his gentle smile back in place and the frown ironed from his brow, he performed his gentlemanly duty and assisted her into the bath.

Alone in her room, he waited, listening to the slosh of water as she bathed. As the water became still, he monitored her heartbeat and knew the moment she fell asleep. Keeping track of the steady thrum of her heart, he began collecting the crystals she'd positioned around her room; moonlight caressed the ones along the window ledge, and he felt the energy swirl beneath his hand as he scooped them up and carried them across the hallway to her parents' bedroom.

A slight hitch in the tempo of her heart, and he was instantly beside the tub, careful not to make a sound; she deserved what sleep she could get. She was so beautiful. He gazed at her long lashes as they fluttered slightly as she dreamt, her cheeks rosy, the warmth of the water, giving her some colour. Lips slightly parted as she breathed slowly in and out, her chest mirroring the action as his eyes dipped lower to pause on the mountain of her belly where the skin pebbled, chilled where the water wasn't quite covering the summit. Throwing a towel around his neck, he reached for her and carried her through to the bedroom, laying her down and towelling the water from her body. Tucking the duvet around her, he watched her sleep. He was reluctant to leave her but finally turned away and descended the staircase.

Kade slipped from the house, locked the door and pocketed the keys. The weather hadn't improved, the misty drizzle more substantial now. He barely noticed as he ran. He didn't have time for the comfort of a vehicle tonight. He hated leaving Dani without telling her where he was heading, but the danger was lurking in the dark, and he knew, without a doubt, she wouldn't let him go without her, and there was no way in hell he would agree to drag her around at night in her precious state.

Hiding things from her was becoming more and more difficult, with her quick mind and watchful eyes, she picked up his tells; never mind the concentration required when she took his blood, hiding memories that he didn't wish to share with her or their unborn child.

Rocketing across the muddy paddocks, sailing over gates, fences, shrubs and sheds; dogs heard him and barked, yet when they turned to bare teeth at him, there was no one there. Time was of the essence. He didn't stick to the roads, choosing instead to go cross country, the most direct route.

The brothers' warehouse was awash with police tape, and a guard leant nonchalantly against his police cruiser, eyes glued to his cell phone, the ping of a game being played loud in the quiet of the night. Kade easily skirted the man and beelined for the open truck which still housed the race car.

A quick check to see he was still unobserved, and he was inside, on his stomach scouting the underbelly of the car for devices. One whiff confirmed their suspicions; a bomb. Daz had attached the device beneath the new car; which meant that the surprise in his voice when he discovered the brothers died in the rally car was genuine. Jumping from the truck, he back-tracked the way he came. Hitting the edge of town, he skirted the CCTV-laden road, ghosting the dark streets at breakneck speed.

A quick time check saw he'd been gone 49 minutes exactly since he'd placed Dani in bed. He had to hurry. The baby's movements had accelerated throughout the day, which was why he'd been forced to seek out Julianna. The birth couldn't be too far off. Poor Dani, she must be so uncomfortable, she wouldn't sleep for long.

Joe's home glowed like a beacon. Light radiated from every room on the ground level. Creeping forward, he could clearly see Joe sitting in the lounge. The television hummed, and Kade stole a look at the screen, chuckling to himself as he recognised the old movie, *Home Alone*. How fitting. Joe was perched on a hard-backed dining chair pushed against the wall, peering over the back of the couch to see the telly. The positioning of that chair told a story all of its own. Joe had a clear view of the windows in the room and the only door. With his back to the wall, nobody could sneak up behind him. Joe was scared!

A quick sniff told Kade the man was alone in the house, and not just tonight. Nobody ever came here. Joe clearly lived under the radar; he probably used a post office box for his mail and purchased directly for his living needs. Why? What was he hiding? This was worth closer investigation.

Stealthily sliding from window to window, room to room, he saw papers on a table, a pair of scissors holding down some cut-outs. Somehow Kade couldn't see him as a coupon clipper, so what was on those pages?

Earlier that night, as he watched Dani doze in the tub, he wondered whether it would be easier for her if he dispatched these low-lives for her. Watching Joe now, he realised it would be so easy to break in and drain the life from him. Hell, it wasn't like anyone would even find the body; he was such a recluse. But there was something else going on here, and he wanted to find out what.

Choices, choices. Did he knock and compel Joe to let him in, break down the door or …

Circling the house, he found what he was looking for. A window on the second floor in need of repair, the frame buckled and misaligned, not worth fixing since there was no way anyone could gain entry. Any human that is. For the likes of him, it was easily accessible.

With bent knee, he assessed the height and pushed, landing softly on the sill, hands gripping the window frame as he slipped his fingers through the tiny gap, snapping the safety lock and pulling the small window wide. Easing the full length of his arm inside and downward, he unhinged the larger window, carefully opened it and climbed inside. Dropping to the floor, he dusted the peeling paint from his hands and clothing.

"I'm gonna give ya till the count of ten to get your ugly, yellow, no-good keister off my property," the tv said, and I chuckled, waiting for the gunfire which I knew came next. I pulled the window to and secured the latch. A distinct breeze still came through the warped frame. Creeping across the empty room, dust stirred, and the wind fluttered the loose paper on the wall. For a moment, he thought it to be ripped wallpaper until his gaze landed on a face, and he moved in for closer inspection.

Dani's face stared at him, not from the greyscale of a newspaper cutting, but a coloured photograph. Her face tormented and pale as she stood beside the caskets, housing her sister and father. Kade stood and stared, shocked. The murder and rape had been splashed across the daily newspapers, those very articles were attached to the wall beside the colour picture, but the funeral had been a private affair, no media allowed. This photograph could only mean one thing; Joe had been there. He'd been among the mourning friends and acquaintances, close enough to snap Dani's grief. Close enough that Dani could have been in danger. He perused the other articles pinned to the wall; all of them pertaining to missing persons, rape crimes, and armed robberies.

Scanning the stories, one name popped up again and again. Gerard Robson. Who the hell was that? The fading print revealed that Robson, now incarcerated in a mental asylum had been charged with several of the reported assaults. Did Joe know him? Was he related?

Footsteps sounded on the stairs, and Kade suddenly realised the telly had gone silent, the light from downstairs extinguished. The landing light startlingly bright shone directly into the room where he stood, and he knew he had a decision to make, to stir the pot a little, or retreat.

Moving closer to the door, he stood, waiting, watching as Joe mounted the steps, his head bent low as he navigated the rubbish on the staircase. *Maybe he'd stay for a quick drink after all.*

Joe had barely made the top step when Kade's voice rang out, "Joe." His head shot up and what he saw, froze him in place.

Kade stalked closer, black eyes glowing, capturing Joe's smoky greys, with his hypnotic gaze.

"Don't move," Kade commanded as he advanced on the weasel-eyed man. "Let's have a wee taste, see what secrets you're hiding." He grinned, and his fangs sprang down. Seconds later, the stench of urine filled the space. Kade laughed, low and lazy as he dragged Joe's head to the side. "This is going to hurt," he said as he slowly pierced the skin and began to feed. Joe screamed a harsh guttural sound, his fear on par with what he'd inflicted on others. And as Kade drank, he saw who Joe really was.

Disgusted and shocked, Kade removed his fangs and stepped back, making sure Joe witnessed the bloodied fangs as he moved backwards into the room and toward the window. He unlatched it and climbed to the ledge. "I'm coming for you, you evil bastard," he whispered, watching fear flash across Joe's face and wishing he could let him remember this moment, but he couldn't. "Forget!" he commanded and vanished into the darkness.

Kade searched those stolen memories again, wondering how to explain to Dani that Joe had been at the funeral. Should he go back in there now? Finish him off? What he'd seen only proved that Dani had indeed been in more danger than he'd first imagined. The man was a monster! No, he'd talk to Dani first; it was, after all, her curse to be fulfilled. He lengthened his stride, bound for home.

Home.

How many years had it been since he truly thought of anywhere as home? Home is where the heart is, so the saying goes, and just because his heart no longer had a regular beat, it didn't mean he hadn't missed that sense of belonging to a place or a person.

Chapter twenty-five (Joe)

Running wasn't something Joe was used to. But after the shock he received at Max's, he knew he was no longer safe. Pulling up outside of his house—he never called it home, there was nothing personal there—he ran from his car, slammed through the front door and turned quickly, sliding the three locks into place.

Looking over his shoulder was a thing in his past, how the hell had he come full circle?

Joe had been the hunter, not the hunted! Now it seemed the trap of his own making was closing in. After three years of being invisible, he'd fucked up.

He should never have fallen in with Jake and his mates. Never should have gone out that night. But after these three long, boring years of living this solitary existence; living the life of the tedious, law-abiding Joe; the pull of his true name and nature screamed loudly at the promise of rape. How could he refuse the temptation to abuse this woman that Jake had described? There was no stronger aphrodisiac for him than fear and screaming. That's what got his motor running. The time for some *fun* was long overdue.

He was just fourteen that first time he lay in his bed, cock in hand as he listened to his sister crying and pleading, followed by the loud piercing screams of pain as his father pressed himself into her. The sound played like music to the young boy's ears as he'd sprayed his sheets in his excitement.

The silly girls at school he'd tried to take out, squealed as he'd heavy-handedly groped their adolescent breasts, making him want more, much more. By the age of sixteen, he had man-handled and date-raped half a dozen girls. Young, stupid whores, so unsure of themselves that they never questioned him when he told them they were doing it wrong.

The more he got away with, the more he wanted. And who was there to stop him? His home life was shit. His father died 'accidentally' in a knife fight after touching up some young chick. Her boyfriend hadn't approved. And then his own mother had kicked him to the curb after finding him jacking off while spying on his sister as she showered. His worldly belongings, what there was, were thrown from his window, scattered across the lawn.

Stealing became a way of life. It was simple and became even easier while brandishing a weapon.

The women he found and bedded, always said 'no' and screamed at him, until he held tightly around their throat or held a knife up for them to see, and then the screams became whimpers as he plunged into them. He was invincible! Or, at least, that was how it appeared until that last whore. The stupid bitch had pulled a can of mace from her bag. One long burst and his eyes were on fire. He reached, almost blind, grabbing at the woman as she backed away; managing to snag the mace, but not the woman. She was too quick as she darted beneath his outstretched arm, ran and locked herself inside the bathroom. He gave up. With eyes streaming and seeing through a haze of red, he fled the dingy room. This run-down hostel was just one of the many dives he used to 'entertain' his numerous women.

Crashing into the walls, he stumbled down the hallway. A door opened just a smidgeon, the lodger obviously checking to see what the commotion was all about. There was no time to think, knowing the bitch was probably already calling the police, he edged his way across the corridor and thrust his body through the open door. The occupant of the room, half-hidden, was thrown to the floor as the door slammed into him and was quickly overpowered by the madman. With streaming eyes, he jumped on his latest victim, elbow pushed against the poor unfortunate man's throat. Blinking rapidly, unable to believe his watering, swollen eyes, he stared at the man below him. He could've been his twin. He sat back, straddling the terrified fellow as they eyed each other. No bloody way, he grinned as an idea dawned and, without thinking twice, he brought up the can of mace and sprayed it into the stranger's eyes. The man screamed in pain, his hands clawing desperately to remove the burning mist drenching his face. Gerard reached toward the bedside table, grabbing the telephone and slammed it brutally onto the man's temple. Silence.

Quickly pilfering the stranger's wallet from the nightstand, he exchanged the ID in it with his own, reached around the unconscious man on the floor and pushed the wallet into his pocket. Then easing the door open, he quickly glanced left and right, before he dragged and dropped the stranger in the hall, then closed and locked the door.

He knew what the old saying, 'in the nick of time' meant when the pounding footfalls of police officers sounded, rounding the landing and sprinting to the semi-conscious man on the floor. "That's him, that's him!" screamed the bloody woman sticking her head from the room he'd paid for.

Still half-blind, the man was led away, pleading his innocents, crying that they had the wrong man.

As the kafuffle in the hall died away, Gerard glanced at the stolen ID in his hand and read his new name, Joseph Matheson.

He'd watched the news as the court reached its verdict on the attempted rape. The jury had listened as Joe ranted, then pleaded with them to believe he wasn't who they thought. The photo in his wallet, proof of his identity, and the appearance of numerous victims testifying he was their attacker, the jury voted guilty. He was dragged away, not to a jail cell but an asylum for the mentally deranged.

Three years. Three long years, he'd kept his nose clean. Gerard had taken on Joe's life and left the outskirts of London in search of a smaller, less populated area to settle. He lived alone. Never invited anyone to his house. The address he'd given his new boss at the composting plant was a post office box number. Nobody knew where he went once he left work. Until he met Jake at a pub one night and listened excitedly as Jake described this hot piece of arse he'd been chatting with. Jake gave him back his life, and as he'd pushed inside that tight little girl and listened to the music of her screams, he felt like he'd finally come home.

This was his life, his destiny. Until the demon had appeared, his black eyes glowing, fangs dripping as he held fast to Jake. And Joe, for the first time in his life, *felt* fear instead of inflicting it. He'd run like a child, along with the others who were meant to be mates, hiding behind locked doors, watching and waiting for hell to find them.

He stepped onto the landing and looked up. Blood drained from his face. The wait was over. He would never get the chance to ravage the sister that got away, the beautiful Dani, whose face was burnt into his brain. God, how he wanted to hear her scream beneath him.

Chapter twenty-six

The excruciating pain in my lower abdomen startled me awake. Reaching for the light, I noticed I was alone. Kade must have gone to feed. Another burst of pain and I let out a strangled cry. "No," I moaned. "This can't be happening now, please no, not without him."

Catching my breath, I struggled to sit and thrust my arms into my robe. Another pain and I groaned as the baby moved violently beneath my skin and settled. "Thank you," I whispered to my daughter and carefully pulled myself to my feet, making my way downstairs to the kitchen. My throat was parched, and swallowing was difficult. I needed a drink.

With the glass in hand, I hit the light switch and waddled toward the couch as another pain shot from my ribs down to my groin. The glass flew and shattered against the coffee table, raining water and glass shards onto the floor. I slumped forward, hands on the couch as liquid gushed down my legs, puddling at my feet. The lounge would be flooded at this rate. "Oh God," I hissed as another pain rocked me, legs shaking so badly, I knew they wouldn't hold me for long. Manoeuvring slowly, hand over hand along the couch, I dropped to the seat, splaying my palms across my belly as I attempted to dampen the rising panic, breathing slowly, in and out.

The sound of a key rattling in the lock had never sounded so wonderful. I could have cried as Kade let himself into the house. "Hey, honey, I'm home," he called as he made his way through the kitchen. "Oh shit!" he cried as he swung through the door, coming to an abrupt halt at the sight of red-tainted water on the floor. "She's coming?"

I nodded as I continued to concentrate on my breathing.

"Give me a sec," he said, moving out of the room as he extracted his phone from his pocket. He came back moments later with towels which he threw on the puddle. "Julianna will be here in moments; we need to get you back upstairs." Placing his arms beneath my knees and shoulders, we fair flew up the staircase to my parents' old room, where we had decided the child would be born. Gently easing my arms from my robe, he draped a sheet over my body. Biting and holding his wrist to my lips, he ordered, "Take a drink, Dani, it will help you through this." Slipping my lips over the puncture wounds, I drank as he continued talking. "The blood will take some of the pain and assist the healing process if she inflicts any damage." I nodded, moving his arm up and down as I did. A contraction hit, long and painful, and I sank my teeth deeply into his wrist, choking as the blood rushing down caught in the scream trying to come up. I couldn't breathe, panic took over my mind, and Kade tore his arm away.

This was going to be hell, I was in hell, and the more I thought it, the more my body felt like it was on fire. Sweat seeped from my pores, tickling my skin as it trickled from my body, soaking the fresh linen beneath me. What the hell was happening? I could barely breathe through the scorching heat consuming me. Why was I burning up?

Just as I thought I couldn't take the heat any longer, the room temperature dropped along with a rush of cool air. Julianna had arrived and broken the 'hell' scenario in which my panicked mind had placed me. A frigid hand touched my forehead. It was bliss! I sighed in relief, my eyes closing as the scorching flames inside were doused, and I could breathe again.

"Dani," Kade said, and I blinked my eyes open. "Drink this, sweetheart," he said, and I saw him take a glass from Julianna and held it close to my face. The bitter liquid made me shudder, but it soothed as it slipped over my tongue and down the blistered walls of my throat.

Julianna placed her cold hand on my belly. I jumped as her fingers walked across my stretched skin. "The child is ready," she murmured almost to herself. Kade moved quickly, lighting candles and placing the collected crystals in a circle. When he was back by my side, I held my hand out as he ran a razor-sharp blade across my palm, capturing the droplets of blood in his hand, before passing me a towel to stem the bleeding. Squeezing my eyes shut, I inhaled, visualising the impending birth and the safety I required from my circle as Kade slowly dribbled blood upon each stone. Breath out and the circle closed. I immediately felt calmer, more in control, as the crystals fed my aura with their positive energy. Turning, I faced a hissing, ebony-eyed woman; her fists clenched as her gaze rested upon the towel wrapped around my hand. I watched as she fought her hunger before turning and scowling at the crystals, a bloodied net she was trapped in until I let her out.

"You need to be up more." Julianna seized my arm and hauled me forward. "Kade, place the pillows behind her," she ordered, knocking a couple toward him.

A scream tore from my throat as my daughter's foot thrust upward, and I heard the crack of bone as pain radiated from the fracture. I ground my teeth and sucked in a shallow breath, pushing away Julianna's cold, unfeeling hands. Grasping Kade's strong shoulders, I pulled against his strength, using him as a crutch to obtain a kneeling position so I could straighten my torso, giving the baby a little more space.

More shallow breaths as I willed my body to the next position. Tucking my toes deeply into the downy mattress, I brought my feet beneath me to a squat. The bed creaked as I moved and my mind conjured up an image of my mother squatting as I was now, arms flung over my father's shoulders as she pushed through another contraction, easing my baby sister into the world. A lone sob escaped me. I wished my family were here with me; but this wasn't the time, I had work to do.

Curling my arms around Kade's neck, I rocked closer, feeling his solid chest against my naked breasts. His eyes focused on mine, and I fell into the deep, dark depth, feeling his concern, his helplessness and his love. He really was my safe place. Losing myself in his gaze, calmed my frazzled emotions, my skin cooled, my heart warmed, and my pain eased.

Contraction after contraction wracked my form, and I panted through the pain, legs jellied. I shook and shivered as sweat dripped, teeth ached as I ground them together, but through it all, my eyes never left

Kades. Hands caressed my back, up and down, around and around.

It was time. I clenched my teeth, jaws aching, tendons close to popping as I pushed with all my might.

Her tiny head crowned, and I bore down, gravity assisting, a quick breath, another contraction and push. Her shoulders, followed by torso, legs, and feet slipped free from my exhausted body into Julianna's hands. Laying the baby beside me on the bed, I finally looked away from Kade, and we turned as one to see the tiny marvel we'd created. She was beautiful, her dark eyes stared up at us, with a clarity I hadn't expected. Her eyes shifted back and forth as she studied us, such knowledge in her gaze, I'd never witnessed before in a newborn, and I was reminded again how very different she was.

With quivering legs set to collapse, another contraction caught me unaware, and I was reminded that Julianna was still present as she gave the pulsating umbilical cord a gruelling tug, once, twice, and as the placenta began its descent, her knife-like fingernail sliced my already-sore nether regions. I didn't understand what she was doing until blood streamed from the wound as she tore the bloodied, liver-like flesh from my body. I screamed loud and shrill; the pain immense. Oh my god, there was so much blood. I knew I was going to die. Quicker than quick, she scooped up the child and carried both my daughter and the dripping placenta to the nightstand. Once there, she set her teeth into the pulsing feeding vessel.

Everything was happening so fast, the pain, the blood. I found myself lying atop the blanket, a towel pressed hard between my legs. Kade's wrist held to my lips as I swallowed bursts of his blood. The pain dimmed enough for me to think.

Shoving his arm away, I cried, "Kade! She's got the baby; she's broken the circle." I didn't know how she'd done it.

Like a whirlwind, he was across the floor but was too late. Julianna severed the cord and was holding it to the child's lips. With a roar, Kade launched himself, smashing forcefully into the old vampire who flew across the room, landing on her feet like a cat.

Kade clutched the child to his chest, cradling her as she began to cry, cooing gently and placed her in my arms. Something was way off. I clutched my daughter close as I perused the circle of crystals. Neither vampire should have been able to cross over; only my blood could break it. And then I saw the dripping trail of red. Clever, Julianna had bled me on purpose, the placenta had been soaked in my blood, and as she'd carried it, the heavy, ruby droplets dripped across the crystals, breaking my circle. I looked at Julianna as she stood where she'd landed.

"Why?" I asked, then shifted my gaze to the baby in my arms and studied the little scrunched up face. She was perfect. "It's okay, baby girl, I've got you now," I whispered, and the crying ceased.

She was more beautiful than I could have ever imagined. Her hair was darker than mine, its silky softness still damp. Her skin was alabaster white. But it was her eyes that captured me, mesmerised me.

Irises black as pitch, ringed with a line of red; disappearing briefly as her long lashes swept over them, only to open again as we studied each other. I smiled as she let out her first hungry wail.

Instinct made me move her toward my breast. But as she opened her tiny mouth, Kade's hand thrust its way between us. Pointed, miniature fangs grazed his hand as he cupped my breast, and then she bit down, piercing the tough skin of his thumb as she sucked to get the nourishment she required.

Duelling sensations warred within me as I realised I couldn't feed my daughter, and yet by simply holding my breast while the child had her first feed from him, Kade had managed to make me feel a part of the bonding with the contact, and I loved him fiercely for it.

There was a sharp intake of breath, almost a hiss, from Julianna, and we both turned to face her. She'd moved closer. Her beautiful face was twisted, not with anger, but something else; frustration. Her lips stained red from the umbilical.

"No, don't feed her vampire blood," she hissed.

"I can't allow her to consume human blood; you know how dangerous that is." The penny dropped. "That was your plan all along. Feed her human blood from the umbilical, which would have stopped her from ageing at all. She'd always be a baby. And you bled Dani in the hope of weakening her so that the child could feed her blood lust on her. You're despicable."

She looked hungrily at our baby. That's exactly what Julianna wanted. Her actions all made perfect sense. Julianna wanted a child that would never grow old and leave her.

"Get out," Kade growled, his voice lowering as he added, "And never, ever come near our daughter again." The threat was unmistakable.

With a last lingering look at our family, she disappeared from the room and hopefully out of our lives.

With the danger gone, the adrenaline drained from my body. I squirmed uncomfortably on the drenched blankets and began shivering uncontrollably.

With his spare hand, Kade snagged a blanket and draped it around both the baby and me. "I'll get you cleaned up as soon as this one's had her fill," he said, smiling as he glanced at his thumb still held between fang and tongue. "Do we have a name for this little beauty?"

Studying the little miracle cradled in my arms, I said, "She was created from both darkness and light, how about Ebony? Ebony Crystal?" I said.

"I think it's perfect. I love you," he whispered and bent to kiss my brow.

Ebony removed her teeth from her daddy's thumb and stared at him.

"Yes, Ebony." He smiled. "I love you too."

Chapter twenty-seven

Days became weeks. Ebony grew more beautiful with every passing moment; she became our entire world. Within days, she had progressed from the tiny baby born in her grandparents' bed to a young child, crawling across the room, reaching for me as I sat transferring images from my phone to the computer. We catalogued every day, taking a photograph each morning and diarising her daily growth and activities.

A trip into the dusty old attic to retrieve the trunks of tissue-wrapped clothing that my father and I had packed away was bittersweet. The keepsakes from both Amanda and I were meant to be pulled out when his grandchildren came to be. I dressed Ebony in her Aunty Amanda's baby clothes, and a deep sadness washed over me that my parents would never meet their first grandbaby, nor Amanda get to cuddle her niece.

Each garment worn but once as Ebony outgrew clothing day by day. From tiny, little booties covering her teeny, tiny toes, zero-sized pantsuits of yellows and greens, to mini jeans and little woollen jumpers. From there it was on to beautiful pink dresses with little white tights and white buckled shoes to match.

She grew!

Her hair, like her name, was ebony, sleek, almost like a skullcap of darkness when she was born, quickly sprouting to cover her ears. Her fringe soon tickled her brow, and those little pigtails which I curled around my fingers flourished into a long ponytail bouncing between her shoulder blades.

We were delighted to discover her love of books, as every evening I would read to her from my childhood favourites. She would point and copy and question, her vocabulary and understanding astounding.

Food was an adventure! She was keen to explore the different food groups; her love of ice cream and chocolate was all very human. Yet with her strong, sharp teeth, she would tear through a chewy bar or to my disgust, near-raw steak. She drank milky beverages like any normal child but to quench her *real* thirst; she would approach her dad and bite deeply into his wrist to drink her fill.

Since her birth, I could no longer stomach the rare or medium meats in which I'd indulged while I carried her in my womb and went back to cooking my steaks charcoal style. Sadly, with no baby to feed, I no longer imbibed on Kade's blood, and so my extra abilities had vanished. No sensitivities to the sun, the clarity of colours dimmed to how I remembered, my sense of smell was toned back, and I realised I could no longer pick distinct scents or hear a hushed conversation.

The bond between Ebony and Kade was impenetrable, and we discovered that even while I'd carried her, grew and nourished her with the help of his blood, her mind was filling with a lifetime of information. Ebony's learning hadn't begun the day she was pushed from my body to land on the soft mattress. It began the day she was conceived; the day Kade's blood first entered her tiny body. It was no wonder her ability to learn, to store information came so easily; she'd been doing it since my first swallow of his blood. His memories, just as I had seen them, were also passed to her. His blood was her schooling.

Ebony and I played in the garden enjoying the sunlight that her dad avoided, but when the cloudy, drizzle-filled days appeared, we would take off on family outings. The parks and walkways vacant as normal humans sought the warmth of their homes.

Sometimes I found myself watching the two of them and envy marred my happiness. They were so much alike with their vampire strength and speed. I felt guilty of the jealousy I felt as he fed her, sharing more of his memories. Sometimes I was a third wheel, the one left behind because I couldn't keep up, couldn't compete in their races. And on those days, I wished … hell yes, I wished I was one of them.

Chapter twenty-eight

Even as we lived in our own little bubble, the world on the outside continued to turn. Seasons began their quarterly change, and the news on the telly had long ceased broadcasting the terrible accident which had ended the lives of Yeovil's two driving heroes.

On our outings, we carefully avoided the small village where they had perished, skirted the area of the auto workshop when we visited the Bay and never discussed the villains within the sanctuary of our home; but I knew that when Kade vanished into the night to quench his thirst, he kept the men under close surveillance.

Sometimes I struggled with the fast-changing relationship I had with Ebony. So swiftly it flourished from mother and daughter one week straight into that wonderful loving friendship the next. I'd never been granted the time to develop a friendship with my own mother as I was little more than a child when she passed, so I cherished this new experience with Ebony.

We shared special moments as we packed up suits, shirts and pants from her grandfather's closet. This was a job I'd been dreading.

Collecting shoeboxes from the floor, we discovered them not to hold what the picture on the sides promised, but photographs of Amanda and me when we were young. I laughed, and I cried as I recounted stories of tricks that my sister and I had played on our poor unsuspecting father.

When Ebony opened the lid of the last box, she whispered, "Mum, what's this?"

I took the antique, miniature wooden chest she held toward me, and my fingers caressed the inscription carved into the lid. 'Angelina'.

"Angelina was my mother's name, your grandmother," I said. "I've never seen this before."

Carefully tipping the lid, two tiny chains tightened on either side to help assist the little gold hinge in holding the heavy wood. The box was lined with velvet and filled with crystals: beautiful coloured stones, each in their individually labelled compartments. Running my fingers gently across them, I was filled with an aching sadness that they'd been hidden away for so many years and a yearning to learn more about this unspoken part of my mother's life. The chill seeped deeply into my fingertips and caused a shiver which travelled up my arm and through my torso. The energy they possessed was negative from lying dormant in the darkness for so long. I moved to close the lid when an empty spot caught my eye, and I knew without even reading the label which crystal was missing. Angelite! And I knew exactly where it was.

My protection stone, worn on my anklet. The same stone which spilt the blood into my sock as it sliced and scarred my ankle that night.

Why had Dad given me that one? Was it simply because of its name, Angelite being so close to Angelina?

Ebony hugged me and left me alone with my thoughts, going down to find her dad who'd spent the past hour checking the buy/sell site for any interest on the sale of Amanda's car. Three cars in the drive were pointless. Ebony could use my father's if she chose to drive. Kade rarely drove, and when he did, he used mine.

Kade appeared in the doorway. "Today could be our lucky day. I've received an email; someone wants to come by and check out the car. I've flicked them a message to come by tomorrow afternoon."

"Great, it'll be good to be rid of the revolting thing. I never understood why Amanda bought something that colour, it's gross." I laughed. "Brings down the tone of the neighbourhood."

He chuckled and sat with me on the rumpled bed. "Eb's making you a coffee."

I shook my head, listening to the sounds of our daughter singing and skipping around the kitchen. "I could do with one. Look what we found," I said, pointing to the box of crystals. Kade leant forward and picked up the box. His face paled as he ran his fingertips over the inscription.

"Where did you get this?" he whispered. "It belonged to Lina, the old woman from my village. My father carved her name on it as payment for the blessing. How is it in your home?"

"Oh, I thought this box belonged to my mother, her name was Angelina, as was my grans', it must have been passed down through the family line." We sat and looked at each other for the longest moment and then simultaneously said, "Lina is a relation of yours/of mine." Chuckling, Kade placed the box back on the bed.

"I can't believe this. After all these centuries, this box turns up in my soulmates house. Is it a coincidence? Or is it something else?"

"I'm beginning to think, something else," I answered. "Kade, you said 'the strangers' appeared to know Lina, and that she was frighteningly strong, is it possible …?"

"Lina was a hybrid, like Ebony, which could possibly make my sire, her mother," Kade completed the thought. "Why did I never put that together before? All these years, Dani, I've wondered how the pieces fit and now, now it all makes sense." He touched my leg where it rested against his knee, sitting silently for a long moment as we came to terms with our discovery.

I reached down to remove the anklet and held it out to him. He looked down at the blue stone as it lay warm on his palm and his other hand stole up to touch the Angelite at his throat as he frowned, waiting for me to explain.

"Do you remember the night you told me the story of your father having that stone blessed for your mother?" He nodded. "It was the same night I asked why you came to my rescue, and you replied, you didn't know." He nodded again wondering where I was going with this.

"My father gave me this crystal after the love of his life died. Just as your mother did for you, these stones both failed to protect our parent. That stone you have in your hand is the one I used in my protection spell the night we were attacked. So, I was thinking, maybe it wasn't just fate that had you running to my rescue, both of these stones belonged to my ancestor, what if they called to one another? You told me Angelite has telepathic properties, what if it summoned you, my protector, my soulmate? My

Guardian Angel?" Kade's head shook slowly, but a smile lit his face.

"Never been classified as an angel before, sweetheart," he said. "Demon, devil, and a few other unsavoury names, but never an angel. I like it!"

Handing the stone back, I refastened it around my ankle before reaching up and pulling his head to mine. "My sweet angel," I murmured as our lips met.

"Ahem," Ebony coughed to capture my attention, and I reluctantly released a grinning Kade and took the proffered cup she held out.

It had been a wonderful day, the rooms cleared and rearranged. My smaller room now belonged to Ebony, Amanda's old room filled with memorabilia we hadn't had the heart to throw away, and Kade and I moved into the room that my parents had shared. Life was good.

***

"Food's up," Kade yelled as he sauntered into the lounge carrying a tray with a not-so-light supper of toasted cheese rolls and three cups of steaming coffee. He stood just inside the doorway and smiled at Eb, and I sitting either end of the couch, feet perched on the coffee table in front of us. "You girls are like bookends. Come on, shift your feet."

I glanced across at my daughter. He was right! She was almost as tall as me now, and her dark hair reached the centre of her back as did mine. We both moved our feet and reached for the plate as Kade placed it on the table. The melted cheese oozed as Eb bit into the crispy bread, and I laughed and handed her a tissue.

Kade took a seat to my left, and I smiled my thanks as I lifted the cheesy delight to my mouth, but my teeth never quite made contact as the television flashed the latest news update and a birds-eye view of Somerset appeared with the headline, 'Body uncovered in composting plant.'

Kade and I glanced at one another. He shook his head, and we turned back to the telly and the news reporter.

'Police discovered a body at Somerset's largest composting plant. The identity remains unknown. Police are requesting information on the whereabouts of the plant foreman, Joseph Matheson, missing …' a photo of the wanted man flashed on the screen, and the news reporter's voice faded as my eyes widened and the cheese roll fell to the floor as my hand flew to my mouth.

"It's him! Someone killed Joe, didn't they?" I whispered, turning my attention to Kade.

"It wasn't me, Dani, as much as I wish it had been. But it seems likely if he's missing."

The anger on Kade's face confused me somewhat. And when Ebony coughed into her hand, and I turned to her, she said, "Tell her, Dad, tell her what you saw."

He blew out a long breath. "Joe's real name is Gerard," he said softly. "He stole Joseph Matheson's identity. The man who raped your sister was Gerard Robson."

"What? Wait, how do you know this?" I sputtered.

"Ebony caught the movie version during a feeding, but the night in question was the night Ebony was born; remember, I was out? I broke into Joe's place and discovered a wall dedicated to rape victims, robberies, and among them, I found a photograph of you. A real photograph was taken at the cemetery as you buried your family." He paused, waiting for my reaction. I felt the chill rush through me but pushed it aside, needing to hear the rest. I nodded, and he continued. "There were older clippings too about a character named Gerard Robson. I wondered at the connection. When Joe came up the stairs while I was reading, I decided I'd find out for myself. I bit him, learned his story and then left him in a pool of his own pee. I'm sorry I didn't tell you sooner, everything kind of got pushed to the back of my mind once I got home and found you in labour, and the rest," his hand fluttered between the three of us, "is history."

I looked to Ebony and had to smile as she tucked into her third cheese roll while watching and listening to Kade recap the story. "He's right, you know," I told her, "life since you arrived, has been such an adventure. The world outside almost ceased to exist. I'm just sorry that Dad couldn't manage to hide this from you, sweetheart."

Ebony sighed and leant over to grasp my hand, fingers still greasy from the melted cheese. "Mum, you know I see what he does when I feed, he does try most of the time to hide the bad things, the ugly things, but sometimes I get snippets. This was one of those times. I've seen this man's story; he's a nasty piece of work."

Still holding tight to her hand, I looked across to Kade. "Couldn't you compel someone to find out the truth, now that he's dead, the real Joe could have his life back?"

The answer came from Ebony. "He died, Mum. The other man died. I looked him up on the internet. He only survived six months locked up; he took his own life."

A tear escaped, rolling down my cheek. "That poor, poor man; another life ruined, and for what? Just so some asshole could get his rocks off." I shook my head in disbelief. Some people were just fucked up.

Reality flowed back into the house.

We needed to discover if the body was indeed Joe's, or Gerard's, whatever his name was, and to determine who was behind this latest incident.

An hour later, with Ebony tucked into bed in her new room, I hugged Kade close. "Please be careful," I whispered as I leant up on tiptoe and kissed him.

"I will," he promised. "I'm going to run past Joe's place, make sure he's not there hiding out and then do a quick survey of the plant. I won't be long." He kissed me long and hard. "I love you," he whispered against my lips and, just like that, he vanished into the night.

Chapter twenty-nine (Kade)

As Kade ran from one township to the other, his thoughts flew back to the night he'd run this path to discover who'd killed the Jamison brothers. The night his life had forever changed with the birth of his daughter. It seemed like a lifetime ago.

The sound of music paused his flying feet. There was a police car parked outside Joe's house, the officer sipping from the steaming flask in his left hand as his right fingers tapped the beat on the steering wheel. Of course! The cops were still looking for Joe and were prepared to wait him out.

Creeping close, staying hidden in the shadows, Kade didn't need to gain entrance to the house. A couple of good sniffs and his sensitive nose picked up and filed a couple of new scents in the area, none which he recognised other than Joe's. Obviously the police had been searching the property. He wondered if they'd broken inside yet and found the clippings and Dani's photo. Would the cops be turning up on her doorstep to inform her they'd found her rapist?

Turning, he ran, feet pounding along the cracked pavement.

The composting plant was cordoned off, police tape fluttered in the breeze, and a security guard was posted near the locked gates of the plant's only entrance.

Kade's nose twitched a little, and he screwed his face up. The smell of decomposed flesh stung his nostrils, even the peaty smells of the different composting piles couldn't mask it. Walking the fence-line, out of sight of the main gates, he leapt up and over, his shoes sinking slightly into the soft woodchip mulch and made his way through the plant until he came to an area where the aroma was strongest. Joe's scent was everywhere, as was expected, but with the added zing of coppery blood. He could taste it in the air, the same flavour which had coated his tongue as he'd read the story of Joe's life. The blood infused with the compost mound left Kade in no doubt that the body belonged to the identity thief. Mixed emotions filtered through him, happy that the prick was dead but feeling cheated that he'd not gotten the chance, after all, to rip Joe's throat out. He moved silently between the towering piles, searching thoroughly for the tell-tale signs that either Max or Daz had been onsite. There! He found it, sizzling through his sinuses! Daz! "Gotcha," he whispered.

<u>Chapter thirty</u> (Max)

Max sat comfortably in his living room; beer in hand, more relaxed than he had been in a long time. He hadn't had a moment's peace since that fateful night he'd come face to face with the girl and her demon and then watched from behind shuttered curtains as his so-called friends conspired against him. He realised that night, as he lay in bed, covers pulled up to his chin as he shivered in fear, that the demon wasn't the only danger out there.

Dani's words came to him again and again. *You will ALL die hunted and afraid.* Well, in that moment, her words couldn't have been truer. A decision had to be made! He would sell out his mates, sell his own soul to the demon in the hopes of redemption.

Conspire against him, would they? He'd bloody show them.

Searching the internet to find and purchase a firearm was way easier than it should have been. And who the hell knew you could learn to build an explosive device by watching YouTube? The internet certainly aided anyone choosing a life of crime.

The driving duo was an easy hit. They were always together. A couple of boxes of beer as an apology had gotten Max through their door and loosened their tongues. He just had to sit back and listen. Casual comments about shutting him up, disbelieving what he'd said he had seen. It hadn't been difficult at all to discover they had been testing the prototype at night. And from there, it was easy to plant the home-made device and tracker to the underbelly of the rally car.

He tracked them over a couple of nights, plotting the best location to detonate the explosive and found the perfect spot where the road narrowed in the small sleepy village. The plan made, he parked up in a side street and waited, watching his phone as the tracker pinpointed the brothers' location. He figured he had a couple of hours' wait, knew their routine of driving to the garage, loading the car and driving the truck to the racetrack before returning it to the garage and heading for home. Making himself comfortable, he'd laid his seat back and turned the stereo up a notch or two. He was startled as the tracker picked up their fast-moving vehicle getting closer and closer and then watched it hurtle past his street, one second, two seconds and he pushed the button on the remote in his hand.

The explosion shook the ground where his car sat, and flames licked high into the sky. Max just sat, turned the music up a little louder and put his car into gear. He grinned into the darkness as he drove away.

He listened to the radio the next morning. The broadcaster made no mention of suspicious activity, calling it a speeding accident. The two corpses burned almost beyond recognition, although a number plate embedded into a tree gave police a clue, confirming the deaths of the racing duo.

When the pounding came on his door an hour later, he froze, momentarily wondering if he'd been seen, but then Daz's voice sounded. Playing the part of an innocent had been almost as exhilarating as the explosion the night before.

And Joe's report of the crash site, his description of the horrific burnt-out wreck and his belief that maybe it hadn't been an accident, that it was the curse being exercised had Max's toes curling in glee as it became clear he'd just gotten away with murder.

Daz had acted a little nonchalant; there appeared to be little to no fear in him until he'd commented about the accident being in the Jamison Mobile, and Max's heart raced a little. What was he talking about? Why would he think it was their new vehicle? Had he tampered with it? The thought that he may have out-manoeuvred Daz only enhanced his euphoric mood. He would have to have a word alone with him; maybe they could team up, make a pact, his soul already belonged to one demon, why not make it two? He didn't have to wait long; as Joe's fear got the better of him, and he had scurried from the house without a backwards glance leaving Daz behind.

"You tampered with the Jamison Mobile," Max stated. The startled look on Daz's face before he masked it was all the answer he needed.

"You blew up the rally car," Daz said, realising that he and Max were more similar than he thought.

Max just smiled and said, "Two to zero, you can bring down Joe."

Two murderous hands met, shook on their deal. Daz would eliminate Joe and then leave town. The two would never meet again.

He hadn't seen either man since the day of the Jamison memorial; all three had stood as strangers in the large crowd, sharing not a word, not even a glance. He lifted the bottle to his lips and took a long swig, the brew bitter on his tongue as he smiled at the newsreader. *A body in the compost.*

Chapter thirty-one

It seems that Kade wasn't the only one skulking in the shadows the night of the grisly find. Returning to the scene of the crime, a man sat, listening, watching, and blending with the numerous spectators surrounding the squad car, gleaning information. The assumed identification of the body was whispered around him, and he grinned, his teeth reflecting the blue and red of the flashing police lights. He knew exactly whose body they had found because he'd buried it there two weeks ago.

Moving away from the thinning crowd, he wound his way across the street, and took the back alleys to the house, pausing a moment as he watched a police cruiser pull up on the street in front, the engine died, and then music wafted from the parked vehicle.

Sneaking onto the rear of the property, he entered the deserted house, stole up the stairs and stood for a moment, staring at the collection on the wall. He tore the clippings down and stuffed them into a duffel. The photograph of Dani was last; her beautiful face stared up at him as he held her in his hand. He was coming for her too. Flinging the bag over his shoulder, he exited the house the way he'd come in and escaped over the back wall.

Still keeping to the shadows, he made his way towards Max's house. The pact that had been made meant only one thing; the trusting idiot wouldn't be expecting him.

Max swilled the dregs from the bottle around his mouth then dropped the brown glass on the top of the growing pile of empties beside him and reached for a fresh one, twisted the top and slurped the froth that oozed over the lip.

Perfect! With that many bottles under his belt, accidents were bound to happen.

With an ever-watchful eye on the street and neighbouring properties, he checked the ground floor doors and windows; all locked up tight.

Standing back a little, he viewed the second floor and noticed the bathroom window was partly louvred. An evil smile inched across his face. Breaking and entering was sometimes just too easy.

Another quick look to ascertain Max was still in the lounge, he moved swiftly to the front door, set his foot on the doorknob as leverage, and hauled his body up and onto the porch overhang and carefully stood, back pressed hard against the wall. Gingerly creeping, one inch at a time, he reached out and up to the ledge and grasped the rough stone, wedging his toes into the mortar between the bricks. He half-climbed, half-pulled himself up high enough to push at the lowest louvre. The glass cracked, and he pushed it inward before hooking his fingers through the gap and dragging himself higher onto the ledge. One by one, he slid the glass panes from their grooves until he had an area large enough to fit his arm and shoulder through, then reaching inside, he grasped the metal bar, unlocking the larger window beside him. *Easy*, he thought as he dropped to the floor and crept toward the bathroom door, peering at the darkness in the direction of the staircase. Muted sounds of the television reached his ears, a guffaw of laughter from

Max and the clink of yet another empty being added to the pile.

Retrieving his phone from his pocket, he flicked on the torch as he closed the bathroom door and looked to see what he had to work with. This guy was seriously into his appearance; shelves of body wash, hair gels and creams, it was what he'd expect to find in a woman's bathroom, not a dude's; although it was going to make his job so much simpler. First, though, he collected the two broken halves of the louvre window. Raising the lid on the cistern, he went to hide the shards. He slid the glass behind the ballcock and pulled out a plastic bag. He grinned to himself as he removed the handgun and popped it in the waistband of his pants then replaced the bag and the cistern lid.

Removing the chain from the bath plug, leaving just a thin ring to grip, he jammed it into the plughole and draped a thick towel along the base of the tub.

Collecting the hairdryer from a stand well away from the bath and sink, he plugged it in and carefully wrapped it in the shower curtain, securing it just above the rim of the bath. He unplugged the taps from the showerhead and switched them on full force; the water struck the towel on the bottom of the bath without a sound and rapidly began to fill. Finally, he flicked the switch for the dryer to ON, opened the bathroom door a few inches and then left the way he came, not bothering to replace the tiny rectangular panes of glass.

<u>Chapter thirty-two</u> (Max)

Max trickled the remaining drops onto his tongue and reached for another bottle, cursing when he found the box bare. The pile of empties had built up beside his chair, and he kicked a couple out of his way as he rose unsteadily, his sights set on the kitchen, where he knew another dozen were cooling in the refrigerator.

Bad move. As he stood, his bladder discovered gravity. Max clutched his junk as he stumbled up the stairs to the toilet. Flinging the door wide and grabbing the air blindly, he attempted to find the pull cord for the light. Something tickled his palm, and he snagged it and tugged, light blindingly bright illuminating the room. Turning to the loo, he frantically fumbling at the buttons on his jeans.

He leant his head on the wall behind the cistern, eyes closed to minimise the spinning room, the beer he'd chugged all night gushed from his bladder. *You don't buy beer; you rent it!* The memory of the girl in the pub jumped unbidden to his sluggish brain; she'd said that before they'd raped and murdered her. "Shit!" he muttered in a burp, easing his eyes open with difficulty, needing to erase the scene he'd conjured in his mind. A couple of shakes and he turned, doing his buttons up and caught sight of his bathtub, the water almost to the brim.

Stumbling forward, he reached into the depths of the bath; the water soaked quickly through his old blue fleece. Fingers wildly searching for the chain found instead the thin metal ring, which refused to stay within his grasp. Changing tactics, he turned the taps off then thrust his hand toward the sodden towel at the base. Water spilt, slapping onto the tiles and soaking his jeans. Gripping the towel, he hauled the heavy material up and flung it towards the end of the tub, knocking the shower curtain, then plunged back in to grip the tiny silver ring. His fingers numb from the cold water and his brain numb from alcohol, he tugged at the plug with all his might as beside him the curtain began to unfurl.

Chapter thirty-three

"Mum, Dad?" Ebony sang out from the kitchen. "Breakfast is on the table, *and* you guys *need* to see this."

Pushing against Kade's chest, I attempted to crawl from beneath him and failed miserably as his fingers rolled one hardened nipple and his teeth grazed the other. A squeal erupted from my lips, "Babe," I whispered as my face flamed, "she'll hear us."

"Nah, she's got her buds in, I can hear the music." He replied and replaced my slick nipple back between his teeth.

"Correct me if I'm wrong, but if your hearing is good enough to tune in on her music, then isn't Ebony's equally as good to hear past her buds and know what's going on here?" I pulled away again, he sighed but didn't resist.

Hand in hand, we descended the stairs moving towards Ebony as she sat in the window seat. Her long hair gleamed a blue-black colour as the sun's rays spilled across it. Her outstretched finger was pointing at the local newspaper. "Check this out."

A greyscale photograph spread across the front page with the catchphrase 'Don't Drink and Fry'. The picture, a semi-detached home, one half blackened with the roof caved in. Leaning closer, I read aloud.

"Somerset hits the tabloids again this morning as firefighters were called to a residence in the early hours. A neighbour noticed flames and made the call,

Kade glanced at the window, the sun was still too high in the sky, and he knew he wouldn't be out investigating the latest death until much later in the afternoon.

"Accident or not, we have to know," he said. "My guess, Daz's scent will be all over the place. And if it is, we need to find him and dispose of this last threat once and for all."

The day dragged as we watched the sun shift across the sky. By mid-afternoon, Kade was done with the waiting. Moving toward him, closely followed by Ebony, I said, "Take us with you." He shook his head and pulled me in close.

"It's too dangerous, baby. I need you here, with Ebony, safe and sound."

"Take care, Dad," she said, going up on tiptoes to kiss his cheek. He stroked the side of her face and pulled us both in for one last hug.

"Please be careful," I whispered and pushed my crystal into his cool fingers. "Take this so you'll be doubly protected." He smiled and pushed it into my pocket.

"Do you really think I need it?" he teased.

"No," I sighed.

"Lockup," he said and left the house at a light jog. I knew by the time he hit the outskirts of town away from prying eyes; he would be nothing more than a streak of movement.

"He'll be fine, Mum," Ebony said as she wrapped her arms around me, and I wondered when we'd changed statuses; her the comforter, the protector? Sadness and pride battled beneath my breast. Sad because I knew she could protect us both better than I; but oh, so proud of whom she had grown into. I hugged her, pushed her back toward the kitchen and locked the door as we went to prepare dinner.

Chapter thirty-four (Kade)

Kade ran as fast as he dared through the town which he'd come to call home. It wouldn't be a good thing for the townsfolk to see him dart past their homes like a whirlwind, there and then gone in a second.

Once he arrived at the outskirts, he switched gears and fair flew across the farmlands. He knew this was probably a pointless exercise, but he needed to confirm for himself that Daz was behind this death, just as he had with Joe last night. It was almost too good to be true that Amanda's story was nearing completion. Maybe once Daz was gone, then Dani could learn to live again. They would be able to travel anywhere they wanted without having the fear that one of those monsters could discover Ebony, discover who her human father had been.

Anyone seeing Ebony wouldn't use the term child, she was a young woman, and what a beauty she was. Her features were so much like Dani's that his heart almost burst from his chest with pride and love for them both. Who could have ever foreseen this happiness—how had he been so lucky?

It concerned him greatly, wondering how much longer before Ebony, like Jerome, decided she looked old enough and felt the urgency to stop the ageing process? A mere taste of human blood would stop the ageing, but the consequence of that would be the blood lust that would follow. The only way to control that hunger would be to leave her human side behind her and to do that; a human had to die. He wasn't certain she'd cope, taking a life. It would surely change her more than just in the physical sense and in her doing this, how badly would it affect their close-knit family?

Kade wasn't stupid; he knew Dani felt left out; was jealous of his closeness to their daughter when they played and ran together. How much she must miss the intimacy of sharing his blood and memories, especially knowing he still shared with Ebony. How would Dani react when Ebony finally decided to change, to become a vampire? It would put a stop to the jealousy, as Ebony's diet would change, needing to feed on human blood, no longer needing him to sustain her. But could Dani ever look at her daughter with the same love with the knowledge that she'd taken a human life? Could she ever forgive this? No, he had to believe this would all work out somehow. But right now, he needed a clear head; he had a monster to find.

Where was Daz now? Miles away, he hoped. The thought that he was anywhere near his family was unacceptable.

He smiled to himself as he thought about Dani offering him her protection stone. He could never take it from her, and besides, if her hypothesis was correct, if she were ever in danger again, her crystal would call him to her.

Entering the town boundary, he was forced to slow to a jogger's pace as he passed some youths hanging around outside the shops. They eyed him as he moved, pushing past one as he made to block the entry to the alley. Kade glared at the lout, eyes glowing, and the youth turned and ran. Once through the alley, he ran across the sports field and followed the reek of scorched electrics and burnt flesh. Coming to stand before the house, he witnessed the blackened shell of one side opened to the elements, the roof having fallen in.

He concentrated on finding Daz's scent. It was faint, too faint. He hadn't been here for quite some time. Had he been wrong? Was it an accident after all? Damn it! He'd been so sure.

Dismissing the faded smell, he closed his eyes and set his senses free to roam. Max, freshly singed, climbed into his nostrils followed by …

Kade snapped his eyes open. No, it couldn't be. He was dead! The unmistakable scent of Joe crashed in on him, and he staggered as if hit. Fear struck his heart as the crystal began its vibrating song against the warm flesh of his neck.

"No!" he screamed as he turned and vanished. He didn't care who saw him disappear. All he knew was he had to save his family. Joe, Gerard, whatever he went by, the madman, the rapist was out there, and Dani and Ebony were in danger.

Miles were gobbled as he sped homeward. The photo from Joe's wall flashed in his mind as he relived the secrets Joe's blood had given up; what he did with her photo in his hand, what he dreamed of doing to Kade's woman. He ran, if possible, even faster. He was wondering how the monster had found her.

His body suffused with fear and anger; he couldn't lose her, *them*. They were the family he'd spent so long searching for. If that bastard hurt either of them, he would pull him limb from bloody limb.

Almost there, so close. So very close that he could smell the sweet scent of Dani's blood on the air. He'd failed her again! Why was he always too late to save his soulmate? He crashed through the door, murder sitting heavy within his still, dead heart.

Did those idiots think he would bow down in fear? Feeble-minded Joe may have done so, but they had no idea who he really was. No idea the things he'd done. It was time to shed the timid identity of Joe Matheson. Gerard was coming back to play! The final scene was upon him, as he put his foot flat, and the car leapt forward, taking him to Dani.

Weeks had passed since the brothers' memorial when he'd last seen Daz and Max. So, when his phone rang, and the caller ID flashed up Daz's name, he knew playtime was about to begin.

"Hey, Daz, what's up?" he asked.

"Joe, we need to talk," Daz replied without preamble.

"Sure, I'm at the plant, don't finish till 8ish. You want to meet here or wait for me at home?"

"Work's fine, this really can't wait," Daz replied, and the phone went dead.

As the last of his crew began packing their gear and clocking out at the gate, he drove his digger to the next pile, picking up a load of organic fertiliser and dumping it onto the dark compost, lifting bucket after bucket, methodically turning. This section had fertiliser added and turned every couple of weeks or so to keep it aerated. The engine growled loudly and vibrated beneath him, strong and dangerous, just like its operator. He didn't hear Daz shouting, just saw the wave of his hand in his peripheral. Giving him an acknowledging wave, Gerard jumped from the cab and leapt the gaping chasm he'd created with the bucket, landing softly right in front of Daz who took a wobbly step backwards.

"What happened to you?" Daz said, catching sight of and pointing to the puncture wounds on the man's neck.

"Passed out, woke up with them. Must have been bitten, lots of biting insects live in compost," he explained. Daz turned white, his thoughts turning to the demon that Max swore he'd seen. Before he could comment further, Gerard spoke. "What's so damned important it couldn't wait till later?"

A little off guard, Daz gushed out, "I think Max blew the rally car."

"Yeah," Gerard sneered. "Worked that out already, so, you think we're next?"

"Well." Daz looked at him. "Actually, we decided that you were next," Daz said and swung his arm. Gerard glimpsed the knife at the last second and danced back, not fast enough, and the blade sliced his upper arm. Sucking in a breath, he held his stinging arm, blood seeping from the wound to drip and soak into the freshly turned mix. He took a flying leap, missed his footing and slipped back into the pit he'd dug. Scrambling as quickly as he could, he tried to find purchase on the steaming compost. Daz was on his tail. Quicker than a coyote chasing a rabbit, he cornered the bleeding man just as Gerard reached toward the digger and grasped the can of CRC, the spray a useful tool for keeping slick manoeuvrability on the big-toothed bucket. Aiming it directly at Daz's face, he depressed the nozzle, and the spray hissed from the can. The knife slid from Daz's hand as he began clawing at his face; scrubbing, to get the oily

film out of his eyes. Gerard slammed his fist hard into his greasy face and stood back as Daz toppled backwards into the hole.

Climbing into the cab, Gerard swung the digger around and expertly manoeuvred the levers, bringing a full bucket of compost to hover over a screaming Daz, and released. The screams were instantly cut short as a load of compost crushed down on him, followed by another and another. Gerard lowered the bucket, its full weight resting atop the pile and cut the engine. Climbing from the cab for the last time, he strolled away, leaving behind him two lives; Daz, and that simpering stolen identity, Joe. Gerard was back!

He made his way across country, heading in the direction of the Jamison's Garage. The shed next door was well equipped for him to hideout. He knew it would take a few days before the body was discovered when the compost was due to be turned again. Picking the lock to the garage, he let himself in, pulling the door to behind him. Walking swiftly to the keypad, he punched in the code and deactivated the alarm. Heading to the office, he collected the laptop and a first-aid box from the cupboard and took it back to his little hide-out. If he was to be holed up here for a few days, the computer would keep him up-to-date with the outside world. Emails popped up on the screen one after another, and Gerard scanned through them as he cleaned and bandaged the deep cut, swearing at the sting from the antiseptic; he noted that a fair amount of the correspondence were offers for the prototype. The brothers' manager must have put the new vehicle up for tender. Crafty sod, bet he'd be pocketing the dosh and doing a runner. Then again, maybe it was already a done deal since the emails hadn't been checked for a few days now.

Scrolling through the saved links, mainly car sales, trading posts, buy and sell sites, Gerard clicked on a link and a revolting, green Austin Allegro popped up on his screen, capturing his attention. No way! Surely, lady luck wouldn't be on his side twice in a matter of hours. It certainly looked like the same car those girls had been driving. Gerard bookmarked the page for future use, knowing he'd need to see this vehicle to be sure it was the same car, and then clicked into a search engine looking for porn, sat back and watched.

Each day he checked the news online, waiting for the report on the body discovery. When it finally aired, he knew it was a perfect crime, Joe missing, the body unable to be identified. He was sure they'd put two and two together and make five. He was home free and ready for the next step. Max!

Offing Max had been simple. Once the newsfeed had been aired, Max would assume that Daz had kept his word. Think himself safe. Breaking and entering was in Gerard's blood, a way of life for him. It had been so easy to infiltrate Max's domain and set the scene. He'd stuck around to watch the fireworks; the lights had come on and then like a lightning strike, the power surged, and whistling softly to himself, he'd made his way back to his hidey-hole.

Rubbed his hands together in delight once the tabloids popped up online reporting the fire and death of one Ronald Maxwell.

And now, to round off this perfect day, he was ready to go and view the green car on the sale site. If it did belong to Dani, his dreams were about to come true. He'd finally get inside of her before reuniting her with her sister. Life was good.

Excitement surged inside of him, sending an endorphin rush through his body. The mere thought of thrusting himself viciously into Dani as she lay screaming, had him rock hard. He'd lost count of the nights he'd tossed himself off as he held her photograph, those grief-filled eyes getting him off faster than ever before.

Opening his phone, he typed the address into his google maps. Unbelievable! She'd been this close all this time. A ballsy little female, cursing six hulking men, and without even lifting a finger, she'd effectively gotten her wish as one by one those men had died, hunted, fear-filled and painfully.

His fingers splayed over the wounds on his neck. He'd told Daz the truth; he had no idea where the marks had come from. Maybe it was Max's demon, after all. He chuckled as he stood and shook his head. What kind of psycho went around ripping out people's throats with their teeth? And then, he laughed again, loudly this time as he thought about the number of times the reporters in all those articles had called him a psycho too.

With Max's loaded handgun holstered on his right side, and a good strong blade sheathed in leather just below it; along with his already hardening cock in his pants, Gerard was finally ready to finish what Jake had set in motion when he'd promised them a night they'd never forget.

Moving toward the door, he nudged the small bar heater closer to the piles of newspaper clippings.

His life's work would go up in smoke. By the time he shut the door and climbed into one of the cars the brothers kept onsite, the lower pages were already beginning to smoulder and curl, scorch marks appearing, and ghostly wisps of smoke began to rise. Ashes couldn't tell his story.

As he pressed his foot down on the accelerator, the car leapt forward, taking him to Dani, belly filled with butterflies as he let the excitement consume him.

Within the hour, he was manoeuvring the vehicle through her neighbourhood. One more turn and he pulled to a stop and surveyed the property.

It was a lovely old house; not huge, but bigger than what he was used to. It stood alone; nothing like the terraced housing he'd been brought up in where they'd had no privacy with the paper-thin walls. The driveway held two cars, although he couldn't be sure if there was a third parked up inside the closed garage. The car closest to the house was the one that caught and held his attention. Lime green, the colour so appalling; he'd never be seen dead driving it. But it was *the* car, he knew without a doubt. Even with a new rear window installed and the paintwork touched up.

Checking his watch, he was spot on time for the viewing. Approaching the front door, his right hand cradled the grip of his gun—he was taking no chances if the demon fellow was about. If he needed something to sink his teeth into, it wasn't going to be Gerard's throat; he could snack on a couple of rounds from his hip-mounted friend. Pressing the red-lit button on the doorbell, he waited. A short moment passed as he held his breath, listened hard, and then let it out in a rush as he heard light footfalls coming down the hallway inside. He listened as the lock turned and a bolt slipped from its mooring. The door opened a few inches, and there she stood. The reason for his sleepless nights. More beautiful than he remembered. Her long dark hair cascaded over her shoulders, past her breasts, stopping at her waist. His breath hitched as he envisioned his fist entwined in that ebony fall as he pounded himself inside of her.

Her eyes were wary, not fear-filled as the last time he remembered, but he'd remedy that soon enough. Her skin was more tanned than he remembered, although in the photograph he'd been studying she was in mourning attire, dress and coat, black on black.

She stared at him, her mouth suddenly dropping as she realised who stood at her door, attempting to control the shock and fear before it could paralyse her. She moved! He moved faster, his foot effectively halting her attempt to slam the door on him. And then; oh yes, there it was. The fear filled her eyes as with the slightest motion; he directed her gaze to the barrel of the gun aimed directly at her midriff.

"Do you really think Daz will come for you?" Ebony asked as we stood side by side, cleaning up the food prep area.

"That's what your dad thinks," I said, shrugging my shoulders. "I guess we just wait and see what your father has to report when he gets back."

Drying my hands, I gave her an affectionate pat on the back. "Supper should be ready soon, pop upstairs and wash up," I said. She turned toward me and kissed my cheek; it was a strange feeling, like looking into a fairground mirror, my 'almost' reflection shown back with just a couple of minute adjustments. She headed from the kitchen, and I heard her feet falter in the hallway.

"Mum," she called. "There's a man across the street staring at our house, do you think he could be the guy wanting to look at the car?" she queried.

"Bugger, I'd forgotten about that. Dad said someone was coming this afternoon, didn't catch the time though. I don't know, I suppose we'll see, won't we, if he comes a-knockin'," I replied and turned back to turn the cooker off.

Ebony continued up the stairs; her hands soaped up when the doorbell rang. She heard her mother's footsteps as she made her way from the kitchen and the sound of the lock being turned.

She was reaching for a towel when it dawned on her; she'd not heard any voices. The absence of a welcome was not like her mother at all. Creeping to the top of the stairs, she looked through the railing.

From her perch, she could see her mother's back and the man's legs up to his belt. She could see his foot against the door as if he was holding it in place and something in his hand that he had held out to her mum.

No, not holding out, but pointing at. It was a gun. Ebony sat frozen, fear for her mother filling her and panic, making her heart beat triple time. She crouched, watching and waiting, wondering, what would Dad do?

Chapter thirty-seven

"Remember me?" Gerard drawled.

"I heard you died," I answered, nervously watching the gun.

"You and the rest of the world," he replied with a laugh. "Where's that freaky boyfriend of yours?"

"In the other room," I lied, and he laughed again.

"Liar, he wouldn't be sitting around while you stand here with a gun to ya belly."

He nudged the gun forward, and I stepped back as he came in and closed the door behind him, clicking the lock into place.

"I'd hate to be interrupted again," he said as he winked at me.

"What do you want from me?" I whispered my concern, not for me, but Ebony just up the stairs. It was silly of me to lower my voice; I knew her vampire hearing would pick up every word, and I was terrified she would come running and put herself in danger to save me.

"Unfinished business, baby, unfinished business," he replied, holstering his gun to my utmost relief, but swiftly replacing it with a vicious-looking blade instead. I backed away. My bare feet encountering the worn carpet of the living room. Should I try and run? How far would I get knowing all the doors were locked? And where would I go knowing Ebony was still in danger?

I needed to stall, give Kade time to get back. Had he discovered the truth yet? Did he know that Daz was the body in the compost?

Stall, stall.

"Um, so," I swallowed nervously, "Joe, or is it Gerard now?" I said and watched his eyebrows draw down into a frown.

"Clever little girl, aren't we?" he answered. "I'm impressed. As much as I'd love to know where ya got that info from, we don't have the time. Quit with the chitchat, I know you're stallin', hoping your man gets back in time. He won't!" He winked again, and I never saw his arm move; just felt the pain as the knife penetrated deep into my skin; blood painted my white dress like a crimson sunset. Eyes wide with shock, I looked down at the blade lodged in my chest, the cold steel burning as the pain took my breath. Staggering, I moved backwards, the coffee table caught at the back of my knees and then I was toppling, one hand on the hilt of the knife, the other frantically searching for something to slow my descent.

The couch was just out of reach, and the back of my head caught the side of the armchair, jarring my neck forward as I landed heavily on my back, and I felt the air explode from my lungs.

The knife-edged ever more deeply into my flesh and the slight twist to the handle as I landed would have brought a scream to my lips if I had any air left to voice the sound.

No sooner had I landed, Gerard was atop me. His crazed eyes wide with excitement, his hot hands squeezing my breasts, tearing the buttons from my dress to expose my tender flesh. Rivulets of red seeped from the wound, winding around the underside of my breast, tickling its way from the torn flesh to trickle and pool on the carpet. The blade vibrated within my flesh as my dress was wrenched from around it, loosening the airlock from the initial thrust, and I realised then, if he withdrew the knife, I would surely bleed to death.

With one last violent tug, my dress flew apart down the length of my body; its full skirt lay like broken wings on either side of me. My panties ripped from my body, and the manic rapist sat back on his haunches, allowing his lecherous gaze to linger on my naked body spread before him.

The look on his face; desire, excitement he couldn't hide as he stared at the manicured triangle of hair covering what promised to fulfil all his dreams as he fought with his zipper and lowered his pants. Poised above me, he savoured what he knew was coming. His eyes attempted to capture mine, needing to see the fear and loathing as much as he required the sounds of my screams to serenade his lustful act.

His body stilled, like a rattlesnake about to strike, his eyes on my face, but I wasn't watching him. I wouldn't give him the satisfaction he desired from taking what didn't belong to him. I stared past him and smiled.

A hand landed on his shoulder, and suddenly Gerard was flying, the air punched from his lungs as he hit the wall and began to lose consciousness. He watched as Dani towered above him, like an avenging angel, her clothes intact, the wound he'd inflicted healed. *What kind of witchery was this?* He thought as the darkness overcame him.

Moving swiftly to her mother's side, Ebony studied the knife protruding from her chest. With each ragged breath, the blade shifted slightly, and blood bubbled from the wound.

She watched as her mother's eyes began to lose focus and knew she was losing the battle. "So sorry," her mum hissed through clenched teeth.

Ebony leant forward, grasped the hilt decisively and pulled, dislodging the knife and throwing it to the side. Plunging her fingers into the hole, she attempted to plug the flow. She needed to slow her mother's heart, to stop the erratic pumping. She knew how, learned from the shared blood memories with her father, the problem was, she was a hybrid. What if that technique only worked for the truly dead?

Bending close to her mother's ear, she whispered, "Love you, Mum." Placing her lips near the wound, she took a deep breath and extended her fangs, pumping the pheromones into her mother's pain-wracked body.

Dani's heart slowed instantly as the pain changed from a searing, burning agony to a dull ache; her breathing became sluggish, and the pain began to subside.

Ebony bit time and again, licking the wound, attempting to close the gaping hole as she'd seen her dad do. It didn't work! Red tears streaked her face as the realisation that she wasn't vampire enough to save her mother's life sunk in. She couldn't save her, but she had at least given her time. She prayed it would be long enough for her father to get here to farewell his soulmate.

Licking clean her teeth and lips, swallowing without thought, she felt her heart kick, once, twice, and then stop. She gasped, "What now?"

The blood! Her first taste of human blood. Her body ached as her fangs shifted back. She had swallowed the blood. Seventeen was too young. She would remain seventeen forever.

Movement across the room caught her attention, simultaneously, Joe regained consciousness and the front door splintered. She moved to face her assailant, and her father launched his way across the room to kneel beside the love of his life.

She laughed suddenly, and it turned into a sob. There was no time; she would grieve later. Right now, she had a job to do. Gerard was slowly gaining his feet when Ebony attacked. Raising one hand, he tried to fend her off while grappling for his gun with the other. Too late, the woman was on him, fast, furious. She held his arms in a bruising grip as he stared into the face of a slightly younger Dani. How? No article had indicated another sister, and he'd certainly not seen her at the funeral where he'd snapped Dani's picture. Where had she been hiding? Who was she? His unspoken question was answered as Ebony tipped her head back and opened her mouth. Tiny pearl-like teeth glistened with saliva, and he watched in horror, as her canines slid down, and he was left staring at two, razor-sharp fangs. Her eyes, so like her mother's, slowly changed, growing darker, until black irises ringed with red stared back at him. He didn't like this answer; this female was the devil's spawn! A product created by the demon and Dani. He shuddered at the thought and then anger filled him as he pictured the demon pushing into the woman which he had failed not once, but twice to experience.

Disgust filled his face as he lashed out, fighting with every fibre of his being, her fangs coming perilously close to his neck way more times than he would have liked.

He thought he almost had her for a second or two when she seemed to lose focus, watching her parents, and then she was holding him again, countering his every move. His body ached from the numerous hits. She was playing with him as a cat plays with a mouse. She was untiring, while his breath came in heavy pants, and sweat dripped from his body. An unexpected double hit to the head and she had him. Twisting him within her grasp, she pulled his back to her front and held him still with a hand across his forehead. The feel of her breasts thrust against his shoulders thrilled him. He was a sick bastard, the rapist that lived within him exulted in the feel of an unwilling body.

Head held fast, Gerard found he couldn't look away from the two lovers on the floor, forced to watch the demon whispering into her ear and run a loving caress over her cooling skin. And then, his eyes widened as the demon's fangs extended and they gently, lovingly punctured Dani's neck, and he began to feed on her. When Dani lay lifeless on the floor, a grim satisfaction pulsed through him; at least he had lived long enough to see her terminated.

"Die, you bitch!" he yelled, not caring that it would bring the wrath of the daughter down on him.

Ebony hissed beside his ear, and he cried out in agony as his head was tugged sideways, exposing his neck. He didn't expect the gentleness that he'd just witnessed, but he never in his wildest nightmares expected the lacerating pain as she drew her fangs across his skin. Shredding, plunging those needle-point fangs over and over, tearing, ripping, creating crater-like holes in his neck, shoulders and chest as he dangled, held easily above the floor as Ebony's bloodlust took over. She was lost to destruction, sparing no thought other than the need to feed, to devour, to tear this piece of crap apart as he'd torn her family. No pheromones to ease the pain, bite after bite, deeper and deeper until she punctured his lung and the blood bubbled as frothy red spittle from his mouth as he attempted to exhale. Finally, driving her face into the bloody mess of his chest, she opened her jaws wide, tongue snaking out to stroke, caress his heart before clenching her teeth through the life-sustaining organ and reared back, separating his heart from his chest. His body dropped like the lump of meat it was, and she spat the offending piece of offal from her mouth, wiped her face with her shirt and hurried toward her parents.

Chapter thirty-nine (Kade)

The sweet scent of blood filled his nostrils, and he knew it belonged to Dani; it was the same scent that had him running over rivers and rocks to reach her all those many, many nights ago; the blood of his soulmate; his life partner and his only true love.

The sight of her lying motionless on the floor, her dress in tatters and drenched in blood, the knife shining red and wet beside her, was almost more than he could stand.

His ears picked the sound of two hearts still beating. Gerard's fast and furious and the other a slow, weak pulse, barely there at all. Dani was alive, but only just. He glanced toward Ebony. Only two beating hearts. His daughter's had stopped. He took a breath in through his mouth, tasting, she was human yet, but not for much longer, the bloodlust would make sure of that.

He barely glanced at the fight being fought between Gerard and his daughter. He knew the man never stood a chance; only getting in a good right hook as Ebony, momentarily distracted, looked at him, meeting his eyes and growled, "Fix her" before resuming the fight at hand.

Kneeling at Dani's side, he gently lifted her, cushioning her neck into the crook of his arm, whispering to his beloved. He looked once more towards Ebony, meeting her eyes, and then Gerard's before allowing his fangs to show, long, strong and so very sharp. He saw the fear on the man's face and knew a brief satisfaction before he turned and placed his fangs to Dani's neck and slipped beneath her skin in a tender kiss.

For months he'd fought the sweet aroma of her blood, fought the allure, the sweetness he'd only tasted once, that night when without thought his tongue had lapped against his hand where her blood had transferred as he'd helped her up. She'd taken his blood time, and time again, the agony of his want pushed well down, never giving in and fulfilling his own need. Now finally, as she lay dying, he could satisfy his own desire, save and re-create his beloved all in one bite. She was his one and only, having never felt the pull to change anyone in all his long years. Sending up a prayer to any god or angel willing to listen, he drew on all his accumulated knowledge from centuries of learning and sank his fangs painlessly into her flesh.

She was so weak; it wouldn't take much to drain his lover. She tasted so fine, and he found the lust for her blood as intoxicating as the sweetest wine. He glanced once more at Ebony, saw the bloodlust in her black eyes, the red ring in them glowing as she turned savage, ripping Gerard apart.

Then, there was nothing, nothing but Dani dying in his arms, her eyes staring into his own, glazed and yet still searching, needing to find her safe place in his eyes once more. He took a deep breath, this was it, the moment that could change his entire existence forever.

One final time his fangs slid into his own wrist, and he offered it to the woman he loved more than life itself.

"Drink," he whispered, "drink and stay with me forever."

Her lips parted, and the first drops of blood landed on her tongue, trickling to the back of her mouth, her throat convulsing as she swallowed. Her mouth widened, begging for more. Placing his wrist against her lips, he sighed in relief as she drank.

His head spun, her blood he'd ingested giving him a high like he'd never reached before. He wondered if this was how Dani felt when she drank from him, remembered her giggling like a drunk teen the very first time she'd tasted him. He'd never had this reaction from any other. He felt intoxicated by her warmth; her taste still danced on his tongue as he watched her taking back the sustenance she required. His long-dead heart lurched, just the one vibrating beat as he gave her life and settled quietly back in his chest.

He laid her head gently back down on the carpet.

Ebony moved to his side and touched his arm as she wiped the blood from her lips.

"Will Mum be okay?" she asked.

Kade nodded and then watched stricken as his daughter began to convulse; dropping lifeless to the floor beside her mother.

"Ebony!" he screamed, clutching the now-still girl to his chest, shaking her roughly to awaken her. She lay inert in his arms and then he remembered, looking toward the twitching pile of meat. She'd killed Gerard and taken a human life, a murdering, raping monster, yet still human. Ebony had given the greatest gift one can give; she'd made the ultimate sacrifice to save her mother. Gave up her life, her humanity in that one killing, sacrificial bite!

Setting her gently down beside her mother, he realised it was finally over.

Three humans had died in this battle tonight. But only one would stay dead.

He removed Dani's tattered, blood-soaked dress and reverently sponged the blood from her body, redressing her in one of his shirts, wanting his scent to be on her body when she awoke and carried her carefully up the stairs. He placed her on their bed, before heading back downstairs and lifting his daughter in his arms. He climbed the stairs once more and lay her beside her mother on the very bed they had both been born on. And the bed they would both be reborn on.

Chapter forty

My head rolled to the side, eyes searching for Kade and instead, encountered Ebony lying beside me. Her eyes opened as I watched, and we lay, staring at one another. Her eyes had lost the red ring that I'd seen around her pupil. Now they glowed a steady inky black for the longest moment before fading out to green. I'd seen Kade's eyes do that so many times, but never Ebony's. I frowned. What was I missing here?

She reached across and nudged my hand. I caught her fingers and clasped them tightly in mine. Memories erupted and worry furrowed my brow, but before I could speak a smile lit her face, and I knew she would be just fine. "Thank you," I whispered, and she merely nodded. We turned in unison towards the man sitting in a straight-backed chair patiently watching over us.

"Welcome back," he said as he stood, a teary look in his eye.

Bending slightly, he dropped a kiss on our daughter's forehead then turned to me and claimed my lips, his tongue running along the seam demanding entrance. I willingly opened and kissed him back.

"Ahem," Ebony coughed. "I'm still here."

Laughing, we reluctantly broke apart.

"Yes, sweetheart," he said, "you both are." And he pulled us into a tight embrace.

I smiled at him and leaned up for another kiss.

Kade sighed with satisfaction. His family was safe.

Life was good.

Death a necessity.

And life after death, well, I guess I'll just wait and see.

<u>Acknowledgements</u>

First and for most, I'd like to say a big thank you to my husband, Steve and my family, for their encouragement and support.

To the amazing women in the Ashburton Writers Group, especially Julie, Stacey and Rae for always pushing me to publish.

Spellbound, for proofing and editing ideas.

Last but by no means least, a huge thank you to you, the readers.

Also by this Author

Deborah Carter was born in the UK and moved to New Zealand as a child. She is a wife, mother of 5 and grandmother to 7. Works full time and spends free time reading and writing. Favourite book genre - vampires, shifters, romance.